I0624029

No Time for Fish Tales

The concluding chapters in the adventures
of E. Pluribus Van Slyke, Lt. (jg), Ret.,
wherein he tames the pirate menace, slays
the evil Cyclops, and secures his just
share of American womanhood.

As recorded by

E. Pluribus Van Slyke

in a world orchestrated by

M.E. Meegs

The Oeuvre of M.E. Meegs

Empyreal Privateer

Virtue at Market Price

Them Shes Be Pirates

No Time for Fish Tales

Hush, My Inner Sleuth

LycophosPress.com

The Byblos Foretold Novaplex

All's Fair, Mrs. Biddle

Babes at Sea

Peddlers All

Dames Engaged

The Fly Maiden's Book of Virtues

The Circensiad

BbyblosForetold.com

No Time for Fish Tales

M.E. Meegs

&

E. Pluribus Van Slyke

Lycophos Press

Northampton, Mass.

First Print Edition 2018

Lycophos Press
Northampton, Mass.

ISBN: 978-1-938710-38-4

To those preferring the fictional life

CHAPTER 1.

THE POWER OF SUGGESTION

I spent five long months as guest of the Nassau jail-house—one hundred and fifty-seven days, to be exact—so I speak with some authority when I describe the accommodations as loathsome: a tiny cell with walls of perpetually damp stone, a single window too high to look through, and a steel door with a hatch just large enough for my meals to be passed in. These meager offerings almost invariably consisted of some form of beans and rice, though once a fortnight or so, I'd be afforded a sort of fish stew. I say sort of because I never saw any actual piscine flesh, only the skeletal remains.

On Sundays, I was given a bucket of cold water with which to bathe and clean out my cell. Not even remotely adequate under the best of circumstances, but especially so since during working hours my labor was farmed out to Mr. Higgins' Abattoir. I doubt there are any particularly pleasant jobs at a slaughterhouse, but having never risen from the rank of chief offal packer, that's mere supposition. I can attest, however, to the efficacy of festering entrails as appetite suppressant. I generally went without lunch on work days, and having seen where the stuff came from, never really minded the meatless diet.

How I came to such circumstances is too long and convoluted a tale to be entered into here. (Worse, to do so might cut into sales of Books I and II.) Suffice it to say, I'd been charged (unjustly) with white slavery and sentenced to life at hard labor. The documentary evidence,

I'll admit, was irrefutable: I'd placed an ad offering a girl for ransom, or possible swap. But what of the case's nuances? Such as the fact that the ad was simply a lure for the Amazon queen who'd crossed over to the non-fictional world and abducted my intended from the luxury liner S.S. *Paris,* a contumelious she-pirate who answered to the name Marpesia. After listening to my explanation, the judge stared at me blankly—never a good sign.

I held out hope I might receive a reprieve from the de facto czarina of the Bahamas, an enterprising woman named Gertie Littko. She and I'd had a brief liaison, and even made plans for the future. Not long after, I ran into a girl of my acquaintance down on her luck. Out of the goodness of my heart, I treated her to a meal and a room at my hotel. All quite innocent. And would have remained so if she hadn't happened upon the last vapors of a particularly potent perfume. *Deux nuits d'excès,* it's called, or two nights of excess. (Though due to its paucity and the girl's reserved nature, in this case it amounted to just one late evening of determined abandon.)

Anyway, by the next morning Gertie felt betrayed and I'd been arrested. A scorned woman is a dangerous thing, but never more so than when she happens to hold the power of life and death over those she perceives as faithless. Just a word to the wise, or anyone planning a visit to fictional Nassau.

Happily, I was on somewhat friendly terms with one of the night jailers whom I'd met on a previous stay in the same cell. He'd occasionally give me little updates on happenings about town. Such as a visit by the pirate Jack Tigue, who made off with that damsel in distress I mentioned earlier. Jack also found time to announce his intention to have me drawn and quartered. You see, that girl—the one I'd advertised, Eugenia—was a childhood friend of Jack's. So his attitude wasn't altogether unreasonable. Luckily, he was dissuaded from assaulting the jailhouse when another, larger pirate airship arrived with the same mission in mind.

The Midnight Sun was commanded by none other than the man-hating Marpesia. When she heard that Eugenia had been taken away by Jack, she became irked—*very* irked. And her resolve to have me dismembered doubled. Marpesia, however, was more subtle than Jack. Rather than laying waste the jail, she simply offered the czarina a bounty: ten thousand gold doubloons. She didn't need to ask twice.

But for once Lady Luck sat in my corner, and it was not me Marpesia received. There happened to be a fellow named Smedley residing in the jail who could pass as my double. For whatever reason—sentiment possibly, a perverse sense of humor, more likely—Gertie sent him in my stead. And I was left to continue my career shoveling offal. (Lady Luck has a pretty perverse sense of humor herself.)

Those two incidents had occurred within weeks of my arrest, and in the months since, I'd heard nothing concerning my own circumstances or prospects. Nor had I even a single visitor. Until, that is, one night in December....

Asleep on my plank, I was woken by a nearly forgotten voice calling from the hatch of my door.

"Pssst. That you in there, skeezicks?"

"Aggie?"

"Yeah. Get a move on."

She fumbled with keys, then opened the door.

"Come on. We gotta run.... *Jesus H. Christ!* What's that stench?"

"Me, I'm afraid. You get used to it."

"Like hell I will.... Better follow me—and be quick about it."

It wasn't until we left the dimly lit passage that I saw her blouse was open. Then we came upon my friend the night jailer. He lay sprawled on a bench, passed out, with a bottle of rum in one hand, and his pants down around his knees. Aggie took the bottle of rum and corked it, then led me down another passageway. Soon we were outside, skittering from alley to alley. When we neared the docks, she headed to a little shed.

Only then did she seem to notice her open blouse. She turned away to button it.

"I hope it wasn't—"

"Put a lid on it. I drugged him, see?"

"Sure."

"I assume you know how to sail a boat."

"Of course. What sort of boat?"

"How the hell do I know? One with a sail. At the end of the pier here. I figure we got about six hours until daylight. Let's move."

It was a fishing sloop. I untied it and rowed us out as quietly as possible. At about a hundred yards, I unfurled the sails. There wasn't even the hint of a breeze. I rowed out past the tip of Hog Island, which forms the harbor, and finally caught a breeze from the northwest.

"Can we make it to Miami?"

"It'd be slow going, tacking into the wind."

"What if we go *with* the wind?"

"Well, Cuba, maybe. Might take a few days. Do you see a compass?"

I gave her the tiller while I looked about. There was no compass, just a couple gallon jugs of water and a sack of foodstuffs she'd stashed aboard earlier.

"Can't you navigate by the stars?"

"Well, in theory."

"Jesus. And you went to Annapolis?"

"That's where I learned the theory. But the sky never seemed as simple as the star charts—too many extra ones cluttering things up."

"Well, isn't that Orion's belt?"

"Very likely. But see, then you have to know where Orion will be on the night of December such-and-such, 1924, at... I don't suppose you have a watch?"

"Pawned it to get the grub. Speaking of spondulicks, my editor back in real New York give you anything for that story?"

"He had trouble believing it, but he sent you three hundred and said for you to get back in touch when you're sober."

"Didn't you tell him it was on the up and up?"

"I did. But he seemed convinced you were hitting the pipe again. Do you frequent opium dens?"

"Nix. But a girl's gotta follow a lead wherever it takes her. I suppose the cops in Nassau got my dough?"

"Yes—plus another thousand."

"So what brought you back to this side? I thought you were plannin' on stayin' behind with the rum-runner's whore-wife."

"I wish you'd stop calling her that. She's just a kid who didn't know any better."

"*Just a kid.* Wrapped you 'round her finger, didn't she?"

"I'm here, aren't I?"

"Why?"

"Just worked out that way."

I told her the whole story: the trip across to authentic Miami; my meeting up with Congdon; Gertie's fleecing of him; my abandoning Clem to Baker; the Navy preparing charges of gross negligence; my visit with Cousin Emmie; the visit to *her* by the thugs; Rutledge's false accusation of theft; and, finally, the real theft of the seaplane.

"I take it you don't figure on goin' back anytime soon."

"No, it was quite a relief leaving all that behind. Albeit a brief one. It wasn't a day later I got arrested."

"I been meanin' to ask you about that. How'd you wind up a white slaver?"

"Oh, a simple misunderstanding."

I told her about my pledge to Gertie, my meeting Eugenia, my placing the ad—and about the perfume.

"Jesus. Nothing simple about that. And again this perfume... Where the hell do I get some?"

"Not sure. Definitely not your corner drugstore."

By then, the sun had risen. I could see Andros Island off to the southwest and kept us running parallel to the coast. About midday we came to the channel which splits that island in two and I took it over to the Great Bahama Bank. When night fell, and the island well behind us, I dropped the sails and the anchor and bathed beside the boat. When I pulled myself back aboard, Aggie gave me a sniff—then sent me back in for another bath.

II

Once I'd met with approval, we unfurled the sails and continued on. It was an unseasonably warm and humid night. We took turns at the tiller, but neither of us slept much. I was too excited about escaping, and she too uncomfortable from the lingering stench of my ragged wardrobe.

"You haven't told me how you spent the last few months," I told her.

"What do you want to know?"

"What you did with yourself."

"Free-lanced. Wrote some for the Nassau rags, and a piece on Lafitte for a trade mag, *The Dapper Pirate*."

"Speaking of dapper pirates, have you seen any more of Jack?"

"Saw his ship come into Nassau.... But he wasn't lookin' for a reunion... not with me."

"He probably didn't know you were there."

"Ah, hell... give it a rest."

"What about *Lucy's Revenge* and my erstwhile harem?"

"I heard they got quite a thing goin'. Branched out into casinos."

"Interesting. You know, legally, I should be entitled to a share."

"Good luck pryin' it outta those greedy paws."

"Is Horatio still with them?"

"Far as I know."

"Well, there is one thing you have to tell me. You must've heard Marpesia cruised into Nassau and bought me from Gertie."

"Sure. Only the paper had it Dame Littko gave you a reprieve outta the goodness of her heart. I wrote it myself. Real touchin' stuff."

"But how'd you know she sent Smedley in my place?"

"Didn't. I heard this Smedley was still bein' held, and I thought I'd interview him—you know, do a piece on the mad Captain Bonnet and his brood of mythical maidens. But that was no go. Couldn't see him, they told me. So then I heard they took him, or you, to that slaughterhouse every day, so I tried there. They had a guard at the gate. An' that damn smell... ain't no byline worth that...."

"You don't need to tell me about the smell. Then what?"

"Remembered that clown of a night jailer. An' how he tried to make me last time around...."

"You really put yourself out for a story, don't you?"

"Ah, ishkabibble. He didn't get more than a peek.... Well, I mention Smedley and he tells me the true story— that it was you in there the whole time. Then the knockout drops laid him low, and I took his keys."

"So you didn't know it was me until just before you came to my cell?"

"Yeah."

"But this boat. You already had it picked out...."

"Well, I'd decided if I wanted a story about Bonnet, I might as well connect with the big cheese hisself."

"So you planned to help Smedley escape, and then contact Bonnet?"

"Yeah."

"And didn't come to rescue me?"

"*Jesus,* ain't you somethin'? The world don't revolve 'round you, ya know. You oughtta be happy I bothered with you. Not much in it for me, is there?"

"Oh, I'll make it up to you."

"Yeah? Share that alimony you got comin'?"

With that, she stretched out and fell asleep.

At daybreak, we discovered sponge fishermen to either side of us. They waved, but showed no further interest. Still, I worried they might mention seeing us on returning to port. I made way immediately, and with the wind in our favor, soon left them far behind.

The next night was a good deal cooler. It rained off and on, and the wind made it difficult to avoid. We huddled together beneath the gunnel and Aggie produced the bottle of rum she'd taken from the jailer.

"Didn't you say you'd doctored it with knockout drops?"

"Yeah, but they float to the top—usually, anyway."

It was the first drink I'd had since my arrest, and once I got started, there was no stopping until we'd emptied the bottle. I dozed with one arm draped over Aggie and the other over the tiller. I hadn't been with a woman since my imprisonment. And over those five long months, I'd thought plenty about my next opportunity. But Aggie was a special case. I really can't say why. Perhaps my brotherly fondness for her.... Or maybe her oft-expressed contempt for me. These things can be hard to pin down precisely.

By then—some forty-eight hours at sea without a compass—I had only a general sense of our direction. Cuba, luckily, is a very big target and almost impossible to miss. What's more, we'd actually stopped by the island while aboard *Lucy's Revenge,* so there was no chance Cousin Emmie had placed it off the Cape of Good Hope, or in the North Pacific among the Aleutians. Barring any unforeseen accidents, I felt confident we'd make landfall the next day.

Of course, it's the nature of unforeseen accidents that barring them just isn't in the cards. This one arrived in the form of a tramp steamer running without marker lights. Fortunately, someone among its crew noticed they'd severed our boat in two. Life preservers were tossed to us and, once the steamer came to a halt, a boat sent to recover us.

The crew seemed mainly made up of Cubans, or other Spanish-speaking islanders. We were wrapped in blankets and given hot coffee and stew in the galley. The water had actually been quite balmy, but I advised Aggie to keep herself cocooned lest her wet clothing give away her secrets. They appeared to think she was male and the longer that lasted, the better.

Once we'd finished our supper, we were taken to a small cabin where fresh, but ill-fitting, outfits awaited us.

"What kind of boat is this?" Aggie asked.

"No idea. Could be just what it appears, a tramp steamer, running without lights to avoid being seen by pirates. They seem friendly, at least."

"Yeah, *seem*."

An officer came and told us in broken English that Captain Esposito was ready to interview us. We followed him up on deck and then to a cabin just aft of the bridge. The captain himself was a huge fellow, almost as wide as tall. He welcomed us profusely, and better still, dispensed the brandy liberally.

He spoke English appreciably better than his mate and his questions came clear enough. I only wished I'd spent a little time coming up with a convincing explanation as to why the two of us were out in a sloop in the middle of the night. There was no chance he'd believe we were fishermen. So I simply played it coy, dropping vague hints that we were involved in smuggling something. He smiled.

"Ah, well, it's lucky for you that we aren't the customs men." He laughed, and I laughed, and Aggie almost laughed. But then he stopped abruptly. "I imagine your associates on shore will miss you."

"Ours is a small operation."

"Oh?" he seemed disappointed. "What about your friends?"

"Our friends?"

"Or family? Won't they miss you?"

"Miss us?"

"Well, surely they will want you back...."

"It'd be a first."

Aggie brought the heel of her shoe sharply onto my toes.

"Ferget it," she told me. "We gotta tell 'im the truth.... Ya see, I just broke him outta jail. Back in Nassau."

"Ah... Now we are getting someplace. Go on, little one."

Aggie sneered at him for the slight, but then did as he said. "You know Captain Bonnet, the mad pirate of Barbados?"

"Only by reputation."

"Well, this is his son-in-law, see? An' Bonnet's offered a reward to anyone who can get him out, see?"

"So you, little one, got him out? How, may I ask?"

Aggie unbuttoned the shirt she'd just put on.

"Ah, I see.... And what is this reward Captain Bonnet has offered?"

"A thousand pieces of eight!"

"Really? That's it?"

Aggie looked over at me.

"Just an opening bid," I told the captain.

"Ah... So if we send him, say, a finger, he might make it ten thousand?"

"Oh, I think a photograph would do the trick. No sense damaging the stock."

"Yes, maybe you're right.... Well, I will see about getting word to him. In the meantime, I'm afraid you are my—"

"Prisoners?"

"Oh, let's say guests. And you, little one—if you find it crowded in your cabin, there is always room in mine."

"Ah... Actually, this happens to be one of Bonnet's daughters...."

"Nymph?" he asked.

"Whattaya implyin'?" Aggie asked him.

"Daughter by Nemesis," I added, sotto voce.

"Ah. But surely she should be worth something too?"

"Well, the truth is, she left home without permission. Might save some embarrassment all around if we keep her identity a secret until the happy reunion."

"All right. I will make arrangements."

"Might I suggest an ad in *Rum-Runner's World*? It seems to circulate widely."

"Yes, but that would take weeks. Better is the bulletin board at the Tortuga pirate exchange."

"Pirate exchange?"

"All hiring has to go through them now. They're unionized, you know."

We were escorted back to the cabin. It was about half the size of my cell in Nassau, and smelled not much better.

"That was quick thinking," I told her.

"But will Bonnet buy it? And even if he does, will he pay a ransom?"

"No telling. But at least it bought *us* some time. Our welcome will last only as long as they think we're marketable. Speaking of which, baring the truth as you did was a little risky."

"Bah. Get me a reasonably sharp butter knife and I'll whittle that fat slob down to toothpick size."

"Maybe. But then what? No, I think we should go along with your original plan, only with me playing the part of Smedley. Sailing with Bonnet wouldn't be so bad. He lives well. Plus, think of the story you'll get out of it."

"Yeah. *If* you can pull it off...."

"Sure I can."

"An' what about me?"

"Well, he's not too keen on taking on extra females. But if you can convince him you're male, and agree to marry a couple dryads, I can probably arrange a berth for you."

She didn't respond to that. Whether out of scorn, or because she was considering the offer, I couldn't be certain. Shebas are notoriously hard to read.

She agreed to share the sole bunk, but only as long as we both remained clothed. We started out facing away from each other, and my thoughts toward her held more or less pure. I felt for her as a sister, I reminded myself. Then she turned, then I turned, then she turned again... and there we were, her backside nestled against me and my arm lying over her.

What was going through her mind, I couldn't say. Mine, however, was pretty firmly focused. And I think she may have noticed the manifestation against her behind.

"That perfume," she whispered.

"What about it?"

"What happens, exactly?"

Without naming names, I described my night with Eugenia at the hotel in Nassau.

"Jesus. And that was with neither of you even plannin' anything? Honestly?"

"Caught me completely off guard."

"But you didn't mind so much...." She giggled. It'd never occurred to me she had the capacity to giggle.

There was no more of the perfume. Not even the remnants of fumes. But such was its power that by reputation alone it could transform a wisecracking cynic into a wildcat of desire. Within seconds we were both stripped naked and I was upon her. I went over her entire body with hands, cheeks, and tongue, just reacquainting myself with her sex's topography. Then she was upon me, and.... Well, without going into details, I'll simply say that there was nothing remotely sisterly about her performance.

III

The most anomalous part of the whole episode came the next morning, when nothing the least bit anomalous occurred. There was no lingering fervor, as with Clem. But neither was there the fretful amnesia exhibited by Eugenia. Only some teasing and complaining about each other's post-amatory habits.

"I gotta use the can," Aggie informed me.

"On shipboard, it's called the head."

"Call it what ya want, I gotta pee."

"Ah. Just two doors down on the right."

"I know where it is. But there's no lock on the door. And I ain't risking some gob surprisin' me with my pants down. So *you're* comin' in with me."

"I can watch the door from here."

"Uh-uh. You might wander off. You can wash up while I attend to business."

There's nothing like sharing morning ablutions with a woman in a filthy lavatory to take the wind from passion's sail. But I suppose the fact we'd never harbored any dreamy illusions lessened the blow. Anyone observing us would think we'd been married for years and long since settled into a comfortable domesticity.

The crewman who brought us breakfast gave me a wink and Aggie a thorough looking over. I thought perhaps Captain Esposito had let the cat out of the bag, but then remembered how easily sound travels aboard ship. Anyone sharing your ventilation shaft shares your secrets.

We spent most of the next day either taking the air on deck or playing cards with the Creole cook. When we neared Tortuga late that afternoon, we were taken to our cabin and locked in. Sometime after dark the ship docked and Esposito had us brought once more to his quarters.

"I thought it might be best if you write the ransom note yourself."

"If you'd like."

"Sure, why not? But keep it brief. Tell Bonnet we have you and...," he turned his gaze on Aggie, "a surprise. Ten thousand pieces of eight, or the equivalent in a certified check drawn on a reputable bank. If he's interested, we will rendezvous at dawn, say, a week from tomorrow."

"That's not much time. He might be up north someplace."

"Oh, word will get to him. He can make it if he wants."

"All right. Should he meet you here?"

"Too risky. Tell him Dead Man's Cove."

"Where's that?"

"He'll know. Where all the drops take place."

"Couldn't we pick someplace with a less ominous name?"

"No! Because that's just what will happen to you if he doesn't show!" He turned back to Aggie. "But not you, little one."

She gave him one of her sneers, but to little effect. When he was through leering at her, he handed me a piece of card stock and a pen. "Just make sure it's convincing—or else!"

I kept it brief, just as he asked. Then, also at his suggestion, I signed in blood: my own. A bit painful, but there's no denying the sacrifice lent the thing a certain piratical authenticity.

While he went off to post the note at the exchange, we were returned to our cabin.

"I ain't so crazy about this plan," Aggie told me.

I held a finger to my lips and pointed to the vent. We draped a towel over it and huddled in the far corner.

"It was your plan to contact Bonnet originally," I pointed out.

"Yeah, but with the *real* Smedley. Now there's too many things that can go wrong. Like what if Bonnet doesn't bite? Or, if he does, what if he figures out you're not Smedley?"

"Two eventualities I was trying not to think about.... Well, if we can get off the boat, we might find refuge at *Le Pélican Débauché*."

"Yeah? I don't remember the place bein' particularly friendly."

"No, but it seems the manager of the establishment, a woman named Clarisse, shares her favors with Smedley."

"Well, while you're sharing her favors, what happens to me? Debauched like that pelican?"

"I'll persuade her I need to convalesce before I'm ready to dine with her."

"That seem plausible?"

"If you knew what a meal with her entails, you wouldn't have to ask that question. Imagine a ten-course barrage combined with a carnal pentathlon."

"Sounds interestin'. And how do you explain me?"

"Simple—I'll say you're my valet."

"Simple. Unless someone recognizes me from the time Lafitte stripped me naked on the main stem."

"Well, either we take our chances ashore, or stay here and hope Bonnet comes through with the ten thousand. And not many men are *that* fond of sons-in-law."

"Yeah, all right. Sooner we get off this reekin' tub the better." She produced a paring knife from the interior of her seaman's blouse. "The cook left this behind at the card table."

"A bit risky to start a knife fight when there are two dozen of *them* and all likely armed with cutlasses."

"Well, whattaya got in mind?"

"I'll pretend to be asleep on the bunk. You knock for the guard, then ask to use the head. He'll follow you, and I'll come up from behind and knock him out. Then we sneak off as quietly as possible."

"All right. But move fast. If he lays a mitt on me, it's toothpick time." She flashed the knife again to make her point.

There were just two problems with the plan. First,

our captors had been careful not to allow us anything useful as a cudgel. The best I could come up with was a tin cup. Second, the guard stationed at the door was the rare chivalrous brigand. He opened the door and actually tipped his cap to Aggie. Then he stayed discreetly behind as she went off to the head.

When he leaned down to retie a shoe, I made my move. I leapt out of bed and lunged for him. He looked up at me with an expression of surprise, as if my aggressive behavior had been completely unexpected. I regretted having fallen short of his expectations, but things had gone too far by then to alter the plan. I swung at him with the cup. He deftly deflected the blow and the tin flew out my hand. The noise of it bouncing from steel wall to metal floor reverberated throughout the ship.

Aggie emerged brandishing her paring knife. Bloodshed now seemed inevitable. But when the well-mannered seaman merely stared at her, open-mouthed, Aggie was unable to strike. For the moment, they both stood frozen.

Footsteps ascended a ladder from below. I ran past them both and pulled Aggie up on deck.

"We'll have to swim for shore."

"Jesus. What smells?"

"What we'll be swimming in, I'm afraid."

She hesitated, but I pulled her over the side.

A busy harbor rarely affords agreeable bathing. The discharge of sea vessels ranges from the thoroughly rank to the utterly fetid. But a pirate port is something else altogether. Body parts—detached limbs, whole torsos, an occasional head—in various stages of decomposition, and in quantities far larger than you'd imagine possible, must be added to the mix.

Aggie passed out soon after hitting the filthy drink. Thankfully, my long training at the abattoir stood me in good stead. I slipped an arm across her chest and made for shore with a modified sidestroke. Our captors shouted at us, but unless they were willing to enter the cesspool themselves, there was little they could do. Soon we were swallowed by the darkness.

As objectionable as the crossing was, I bypassed the nearest landings in case the brigands managed to pursue us along shore. We finally beached beside what turned out to be a primitive brewery. Given the predilection of pirates for all things alcoholic, security seemed surprisingly lax. But I soon determined this was due to the inferiority of the product. As beer, it was pretty sorry stuff. As a rinse for the putrid brine of the harbor, however, it was quite serviceable.

Aggie began to stir with the fourth bucket.

"What the hell are you doin'?"

"Trying to freshen you up. You passed out on hitting the water."

"Christ. Didn't smell like water. An' whatta we do now, all soaked in beer?"

"Blend in. Pirates generally come soaked in the beverage of their choice. But I suggest we wait a few hours for things to get going. It's still early, pirate-time."

It was a sound idea. But a visitor to a pirate port must be prepared for contingencies, and sound ideas only occasionally go off as expected. As it happened, the brewmaster and his men had only been taking a short break. When on their return he saw that I'd poured out several hogsheads of his workmanship, he became vexed.

"That was a special anniversary batch!"

"Anniversary?"

"The sacking of New York!"

"I didn't realize pirates had sacked New York."

"Well, partial sacking. Once the bars open up, it's hard to keep the men focused."

"Listen, sorry for the damage. We had a bit of an emergency. Love the bouquet, by the way."

My compliment fell well short of pacifying him. He wasn't very large, nor were his cronies. But being pirate brewers, they did manage to menace quite convincingly. Maybe it was the sparsity of teeth, or the myriad scars. Or maybe the way they wielded their cutlasses like crazed killers bent on vengeance.

Had their blades not already been dripping in blood, I might have steeled myself to offer some resistance. However, the very freshness of the gore argued against such a course. For a moment, I feared Aggie might make some brash move with her paring knife. But she raised her arms in surrender even more quickly than I did. And as you well know, I'm no slouch when it comes to surrendering.

"You may be interested to learn I'm the son-in-law of mad Captain Bonnet."

"Bonnet? That son of a bitch! Hell, I'm his son-in-law too. An' I ain't too damn happy about it!"

"No? Bad match?"

"Married me to Alecto, he did."

"Alecto? I don't think I remember her."

"One of the Furies, he tells me. Well, why not, I think? What could be hotter than one of the Furies? And she's plenty hot-lookin', let me tell ya."

"Sounds promising."

"Sure it does—'til ya find out she's the embodiment of implacable anger!"

"Implacable anger?"

"Punisher of transgressions—*moral* transgressions. Now what kind of a wife is that for a pirate?"

"Ah. Your point's well taken. But I'm sure I can arrange for a trade-in. How about a naiad or two? Or an oceanid—fit in with the nautical theme."

"Fat chance. You want to be the one to tell Alecto I'm tradin' her in? Girl tears my head off for leavin' the toilet seat up."

"Does that count as a moral transgression?"

"Does in our house!"

"Well, you have my sympathies. But surely a thousand pieces of eight would ease the pain some."

"A thousand?"

"Yes, as soon as Father-in-law arrives. Consider it a partial refund, and payment for your fine brew. In the meantime, perhaps you could take us to *Le Pélican Débauché*. I happen to be a friend of the manager."

"What, lookin' like that?"

"What do you mean?"

"They got a dress code now. Real swanky."

"Is there much demand for a swanky nightspot in a pirate port?"

"We ain't all as crass as people make out. Say, I don't suppose you could put in a word for me with your friend? I got a Belgian-style wheat that goes swell with the haughty cuisine they're servin' nowadays."

"Well, I'll tell you what. Take us somewhere where we can bathe and get some fresh duds, and I'll see what I can do."

"Yeah, all right."

He brought us to his own home. Luckily, the little woman was out shopping, or punishing moral transgressors, depending which was on the docket that evening. We showered, then he shared his plenteous closet with us. Frankly, I've never looked my best in a violet silk blouse. But when in Rome....

Chapter 2.

The Lull Before the Storm

Anxious to make points with a lucrative prospect, the pirate-brewer brought us to *Le Pélican Débauché* and requested an audience with Clarisse, the establishment's ravenous manager.

I would never have recognized the place. The exterior had been completely done over, and the primitive wooden sign replaced by an animated one of flickering neon. Quite an improvement—though not for the unfortunate pelican. Its fate was preordained.

We were sent to the kitchen entrance, and there met by one of Clarisse's ornately costumed footmen. The brewer was told to leave a sample with the kitchen steward.

"You, Mr. Smedley, may follow me. Alone."

"Wait here," I told Aggie.

"Just don't forget where you left me."

I was taken to an office two floors above. Clarisse greeted me from behind a large desk. She was still dressed in the style of an eighteenth-century courtier, but now wore reading glasses. Laid out before her were what looked like ledgers.

"Sit down, my dear. I heard about your escape from Nassau."

"News travels fast."

"Oh, yes. You know how gossipy pirates are. But I also heard you were being ransomed. How did Esposito let you slip through his hands?"

"We jumped ship. I thought perhaps you might provide us a temporary refuge."

"We?"

"A young associate who helped me make my exit from Nassau."

"Well, if I help you, *I'll* be expecting a gift from your father-in-law—though we needn't call it a ransom."

"Don't worry, I'll see you're made whole."

"And I must warn you—no more late-night dinners. I've had to renovate my reputation along with the Pelican. I'm married now." She flashed an outsized diamond on her ring finger, then tapped her tummy. "With a bun in the oven."

"Congratulations, on both counts."

"I've a cottage up in the hills above town. You can hide out there. You'll find everything you need—food, clothing. But stay clear of my Henri."

"Your husband?"

"Yes—and insanely jealous."

"Well, if it will make things any easier, my young associate is actually female...."

"Oh, so you were going to toy with my affections, just for a place to hide out from La Baza."

"La Baza? Not the Cyclops?"

"Yes. Esposito works for him. Didn't you know?"

"No. He neglected to mention it. Do you think we'll be safe in the cottage?"

She shrugged. "As safe as anywhere. I heard your lookalike was sold to Marpesia."

"Yes, I heard that too. Any idea what became of him?"

She shrugged again. "I doubt anything good. He swindled me, you know. He and your sister-in-law, Avarice."

"Yes, Bonnet as well. But it looks as if you've recovered nicely."

"Well, the greedy one and I have come to terms. More money for everyone now."

"Do you see her often?"

"The last day of the month, like clockwork. Do you feel confident Bonnet will pay?"

"Let's say I'm optimistic. There is one problem, however. Esposito will be waiting at the drop, with or without me."

"Yes. And La Baza, too. I'll have to think about how to deal with that."

She rang a little bell and the footman returned.

"You are to take this man and his friend to the cottage—and tell no one."

He made a little bow, then led me out of the room.

We found Aggie in conference with one of the chefs. She flirted with him in perfect French, and he responded by popping morsels of whatnot in her mouth.

"We're on the lam, remember? Best not to make a spectacle of yourself."

"You fix things with Madame?"

"Yes. This fellow is going to escort us to a refuge."

Outside, the footman called for a carriage. We rode three or four miles, then we left the carriage behind and he led us along a path, then another, and another. We'd traveled three-quarters around a circle. I assumed just to make sure we weren't followed.

The cottage itself was shrouded in vines, and from the outside looked hopelessly decrepit. But inside, it felt remarkably homey. The footman had us close all the curtains, then lit a kerosene lamp. There were just three modest rooms below and a sort of bedroom loft above. The plumbing consisted of a hand pump in the kitchen and an outhouse in back.

"Don't leave the house," the footman told us.

"Except to…"

"Yes, except to… There is food here, and I will bring more in a few days. You may make a fire to cook, but only at night. And make sure no lights can be seen from the windows."

"All right. Thank you."

Once he snuck off into the night, I looked around for some refreshment. In a cubbyhole beneath the stairs, I discovered a small wine cellar. We toasted our good luck, then toasted Clarisse, then each other, then anyone else we could think of. By daylight, we'd put a healthy dent in the stock. Then we stumbled upstairs and passed out.

When I woke, about noon, Aggie lay with her head braced on one arm. She was staring at me.

"Why're you looking at me like that?"

"Just trying to decide if I could get used to you."

"Any decision?"

"No."

I spent the next hour letting her try me on for size. There were no complaints. A little laughter when things weren't going quite as planned, but no complaints. We breakfasted on biscuits and wine, and I told her about Esposito working for La Baza.

"The rum-running bastard whose whore-wife you stole? Twice?"

"Yes, him. But I wish you wouldn't—"

"Yeah, I know. You wanna pretend you met her on a church picnic. Didn't you say you poked his one eye out?"

"Not poked out, exactly. And it turns out his other eye just suffers from conjunctivitis."

"Shouldn't keep a patch on it then."

"So he's been told. He finds the pink-eye embarrassing."

"Christ. They're the worst."

"Who?"

"Vain tyrants. Can never forget a slight. I wonder if it's safe, hanging out with you."

Her quizzical look led me to think she wasn't speaking solely in reference to La Baza. But she didn't wait for a response. She went into the kitchen and washed her hair in the sink.

We didn't talk much that afternoon. Aggie spent it altering some of Clarisse's things to fit herself. When it got dark I made a fire in the stove and we prepared a proper meal. After we finished, Aggie read to me from a French novel she found. I was lost pretty quickly, but her rendition kept me riveted just the same. She put a lot of passion into it, and it wasn't long before I was feeling pretty warm myself. We didn't make it upstairs that night.

In the morning, I asked her to explain the book's plot.

"Plot? Near as I can tell, it's a how-to book on raising swine."

"Raising swine?"

"Yeah. But in French, even washing your pig sounds like a lurid night in the boudoir. 'Long as you know how to tell the story. Speaking of which, I can't believe you left mine behind in New York."

"Sorry, there was a lynch mob interested in interviewing me and I left town in something of a hurry. But between the two of us, we should be able to come up with something just as good."

After we'd dined on leftovers and cold coffee, I sought out pen and paper. We had great fun assembling the combined tale, each of us able to fill blanks in the other's story. The only times things became contentious were those episodes that we experienced together. When I suggested she'd seemed jealous of Clem, she flung a wine bottle at my head. And, I might add, quite accurately.

Once it got dark, I made another fire in the stove. The coffee had just come to a boil when Aggie grabbed my arm.

"What was that?" she whispered.

"Just steam escaping."

"No, you gink. Something outside."

I moved the coffee off the stove and she snuffed out the lamp. Then we moved to the curtained window. It was only after a full minute we heard a twig break.

"We gotta be ready for him," she said.

"Who?"

"La Baza! Who else? Or at least one of his henchmen."

"How would they find out where we are?"

"*How do I know?*"

"It's probably just the footman."

"Why wouldn't he just knock?"

"Good point. Maybe we should arm ourselves."

"I'm set." She flashed the razor I'd shaved with earlier. "You grab something and guard the other room."

With the curtains drawn and the lamp out, it was dark as pitch. Rather than paw around for a knife, I picked up an iron skillet, then felt my way into the other room. Another few minutes passed. Then another twig broke outside. My heart was pounding. If it *was* La Baza out there, I wouldn't stand a chance—particularly if his conjunctivitis had cleared up.

I positioned myself by the door so I'd have a clean shot at anyone entering. When he instead came crashing through the window behind me, I had to turn about quickly. The room was all in shadows, but I sensed someone rising from the floor and swung the pan in his direction....

II

"Ow!"

A single syllable—and yet somehow enough to strike a note of familiarity. I'd readied another stroke, but now held back.

"Who's there?" I asked.

"Me, boss. Horatio!"

By then Aggie had entered the room with a lamp in one hand and the razor in the other.

"What're *you* doin' here?" she asked.

"Clarisse sent me. To tell you to be on the lookout. La Baza's in town."

"Why didn't you just knock?"

"Couldn't find the door."

"Well, you might've said something before crashing through the window."

"I was tryin' to see if this was the right place. Didn't want to barge in on someone and end up with a lump on my head."

"Sorry. We thought *you* were La Baza."

I gave him a chair and poured us all some wine.

"Did you see the Cyclops yourself?"

"Sure—goes to the same barber."

"Is he still wearing that eye patch?"

"On the other eye now. Says you scratched his eye with that stick."

"Did you speak with him?"

"I was waitin' while he was in the chair. Must be a regular, 'cause the barber asked him about the patch bein' on a different eye. Chatty fellow."

"La Baza?"

"The barber. I don't think he likes you."

"I've never been to a barber in Tortuga."

"I meant La Baza."

"Well, I can't say I'm surprised. Is he hoping to get the ransom from Bonnet?"

"I think maybe he figured out you're not Smedley, you're you."

"What makes you think that?"

"Said somethin' about cuttin' you to pieces. Says you raped his woman."

"That's slander! I never forced myself on her. She couldn't wait to be rid of him."

"I think he meant it in the pirate sense: you took her against *his* will. Her opinion don't matter."

"Same with the classical sense," Aggie interjected. "Paris's taking of Helen is usually called a rape—even if she didn't seem to mind too much."

"That the face that launched a thousand ships?" he asked.

"Depends who you're asking. Shakespeare says it was her *price* that launched a thousand ships—bit of a whore in his version."

"An' this Paris, he was a pirate?"

"Trojan prince. But in those days, they all had their piratical moments."

"Sure, who doesn't? By the way, where's Clem?" he asked me.

"Well... I left her in a sort of... other world."

"Ah, the one you all come from? That's good—might

be the one place he can't catch up to her."

"I certainly hope so. How'd you come to leave the employ of my gentle wives?"

"Got sacked. And they weren't too gentle about it."

"Any particular reason?"

"Not vicious enough, the greedy one said. Albertson, too."

"That's ironic. Then who's manning the ship?"

"She got a couple dozen ant-men. Mail-order from Greece."

"Ant-men?"

"Myrmidons. Fanatical butchers from Thessaly," Aggie explained. "Never questioned an order. Fought with Achilles at Troy."

"They're the ones. Come with a guarantee."

"Hmm. Did the ladies speak of me at all?"

"Oh, yes. You're the one thing they all agree on."

"Agree on in what way?"

"How they gonna execute you. Starts with you being flayed by Wrath.... No, that ain't right... *flogged* by *Av'rice*.... The flayin' by Wrath comes later."

"Let's save the rest. Wouldn't want to spoil the surprise. Does seem a little unfair. After all, they're the ones who abandoned *me* back in the Bahamas."

"Well, didn't take long for them to figure out you tricked them."

"Served 'em right.... So now you're working for Clarisse?"

"She gave me a job as a croupier. An' Mattie's makin' her some maternity outfits in the old style—lots of brocade."

"One thing I don't get," Aggie said. "How'd you know he wasn't Smedley?"

"Well, when the cook described the girl he came with, I figured it had to be my old boss, and you two finally hooked up."

"What do you mean, finally hooked up?" I asked.

"Oh, Mattie an' me saw it coming before you even got aboard *Lucy*."

"Whattaya mean? You'd never met him."

"Met you, though. Girl pays ten thousand in jewels for some fellow she says she don't like...."

"Does Clarisse know?"

"Does now. 'Fraid I let the cat out of the bag. Didn't know you were back to pretendin' to be Smedley. That mean the Amazons got *him?*"

"Yes. Though whether they still have him, I don't know. Can we trust Clarisse?"

"Well, if you can fool Bonnet, and she can get her hands on the money, she don't care who you pretend to be."

"Has Clarisse come up with a plan for evading La Baza at the drop?"

"Well, one plan. But you won't like it."

"What?"

"Send Aggie to Port Royal as a decoy. If he hears she's there, he'll figure you're there too. An' without you, no point goin' to the drop."

"Too risky. What if he catches up with her?"

"That wouldn't be good."

"Ah, ishkabibble. He shows up, I'll carve out both eyes an' his nose besides." She flashed her razor.

"Up to you," Horatio told her. "There's an airship leaving for Port Royal in the mornin'. Idea is, we make sure people see you both get on board. Then the boss here leaves the ship before it takes off. When you get to

Port Royal, you let yourself be seen—just enough to draw La Baza. Then Clarisse takes the boss to Dead Man's Cove and hands him off to Bonnet. When La Baza hears about it, he'll make for home. Unless—"

"Unless he feels a need to wreak vengeance," I added.

"Yes. Unless that."

"And even if he doesn't, what happens to Aggie?"

"Up to her, I guess."

"I'll land on my feet," Aggie said. "But I want two thousand for my trouble—in advance."

"I'll tell Clarisse, we'll see what she says. Either way, I'll be back just before dawn. Assumin' I can find my way back to town...."

He left soon after and I poured Aggie and myself another glass of wine.

I don't pretend to have any special insight into the female psyche, but one thing was sure: I was being tested. And the two thousand Aggie had asked for was just part of the test. You see, if she agreed to go as a decoy for nothing, even someone as shameless as me would be shamed into forbidding it. But by making it appear she was motivated by profit, or at least considered it in her calculations, she gave me an out: I could fool myself into accepting her act as pure self-interest.

Unfortunately, her intention was so transparent, I couldn't fool myself. No matter how hard I tried.

"I've been thinking it over, and as senior partner, I'm nixing the plan."

"Senior partner?"

For some perverse reason, I'd come to enjoy seeing her livid—just so the razor wasn't close at hand.

"Look, we both stand a better chance working together. Help me hoodwink Bonnet, and we might be able to take over his whole operation. Be worth a lot more than two thousand."

"Yeah? Maybe.... 'Course, you'll probably get a replacement harem out of it either way. I remember you goin' on about those naiads, and dryads, and whatnads...."

"Mere girls. And what have you got to lose? I'm the one taking the risk."

"Yeah, all right—but we don't make any vows."

"Should I swear to it?"

"Jerk."

I opened another bottle so we could drink on it. After two more glasses, Aggie became uncharacteristically dreamy-eyed. She started to say something. Then bit her lip. When I started to get up, she grabbed my arm.

"Tell me about that perfume again."

This time I related my experience with Pride and Wrath together. And in detail. At first she just listened, her eyes closed, and her mouth emitting little noises of commentary. Then, just as I finished relating one notably selfless act on my part, I noticed she'd pulled up the skirt of her dress well above her knees. Never before then had I imagined Aggie as a temptress. But my image of her was evolving quickly.

I won't claim we recreated that earlier bout round for round. After all, there was just one of her. And she had nowhere near a Sin's physical strength. Holding some of those positions required a stamina Aggie simply didn't have in her. Offsetting those disappointments, however, she also lacked a Sin's proclivity for inflicting pain. In sum, I'd call it a congenial variation on the theme.

We were woken many hours later by Horatio. It being well after sunrise, he apologized.

"Got lost again. Looks different in daylight."

"Listen," I told him, "we've decided not to take the risk, sending Aggie to Port Royal."

"Hoped you'd say that."

"When'd you become such a sentimentalist?" she asked him.

"Oh, me? Well, I've always been a sucker for a happy ending."

"Well, better wait 'til this is over before you start weepin' for joy."

He'd brought a sack of food, including half a ham, and we shared a cold breakfast with him. When he prepared to leave, Aggie stopped him.

"You never told us what your boss said about givin' me that two thousand."

"No, I didn't." He winked at her and crept out into the daylight.

"What kind of queer answer was that?" she asked me.

"Not sure. Maybe he never asked her."

"Or maybe she said no...."

"What's it matter?"

She shrugged—but the indifference seemed feigned.

She was one strange sheba, all right.

III

We spent the next few days much as we had the previous ones. Though with time, the monotony of our existence became increasingly less bearable. What had seemed a cozy cottage began to feel like a prison. Not surprisingly, the lovemaking turned sporadic, and appreciably less athletic. This latter development, however, didn't result in a more restful stay. Like a fretful housewife, Aggie began hearing noises, usually just after I'd managed to fall asleep. And anytime she heard a noise, it had to be investigated. Taken together, a casual observer might say our lives had been reduced to the tedious existence commonly referred to as married life.

Of course, that casual observer would be sorely mistaken. He'd apparently failed to glom onto the fact that we were headed for some very risky business involving some very ruthless villains—and taking place at the very inauspiciously named Dead Man's Cove. Tedium is a quite manageable problem when disembowelment lies just over the horizon.

The day before the grand event—when none of us had come up with a way to distract La Baza—I sent a request to Clarisse that we call the thing off until the Cyclops lost interest. She sent her emphatic one-word reply via a pair of well-armed thugs she'd assigned to watch over us until the transaction was completed. As you may have guessed, that word was no.

Thugs are pretty easy to come by in a pirate port. So a buyer can afford to be selective. Clarisse exercised this privilege by finding two of the most forbidding goons I'd yet come across. It wasn't merely the fact that they were huge and muscular—though they were that. Or the fiery tempers they exhibited whenever we failed to comply with the proper alacrity or obsequiousness to some instruction they'd given.

I suppose if I had to lay it to just one trait it would be their choice of conversational topic. It rarely strayed from three main themes: pillaging, raping, and human dismemberment. And for these brutes, there wasn't much ambiguity in their use of the word rape.

It's possible, I imagine, to construct a humorous anecdote from the forthright sacking of some wealthy port town. Schadenfreude is, after all, a normal, healthy sensation. With the latter two topics, however, one has crossed a line. Your average pirate might consider it a very thin line. But only the cruelest, most debased of them would deny it altogether. Unfortunately, that's the camp from which these two fellows hailed.

Aggie and I spent that last night in each other's arms. But such was our trepidation at what the morrow would bring, no thought was given to amorous coupling. (Though to be honest, the celibacy was at least partly attributable to the fact that one or the other of the thugs stood watch over us the entire night.)

The rendezvous at Dead Man's Cove had been set for dawn. But there was some confusion the next day when we realized it hadn't been made clear whether this meant *normal* dawn—namely, sunrise—or *pirate* dawn. For those late risers, dawn generally equated to high noon. As it was, packing took longer than we expected and we didn't get to the cove until well after eleven.

Clarisse and a small entourage of auxiliary ruffians met us at a clearing along the shore.

"So glad you could make it," she said.

I didn't mind so much her laughing as she said it, but I couldn't see why she went on for so long—not until I noticed the fellow standing at a lectern a few yards away. He reminded me of a common type encountered in my youth: the country auctioneer. Beside him was a platform with a post running up the middle. And attached to this post was a pair of shackles.

A half-second after my noticing the shackles, I'd been attached to them.

"What fiendishness is this?" I shouted.

"Oh, come now. Isn't it only natural I make the best use of you possible?"

"But selling a fellow human has to be the most despicable act imaginable!"

I'd chosen my words poorly. Especially given the crowd. In no time, the assembly came up with quite a long list of alternatives, all graphically described, and all, admittedly, far more despicable.

"You, my dear, may choose," Clarisse said to Aggie. "Go with him, or stay here with us."

Aggie broke free of the ruffian holding her and joined me on the platform. It was quite the noble display. Though frankly they'd made it rather an easy choice, given their encyclopedic knowledge of acts despicable.

By then La Baza was approaching with a small navy of steam launches, each one manned by a dozen or so of his own ruffians. There was no sign of Bonnet, but just a minute before the hour we heard the sound of an airship approaching. If my dear father-in-law were to outbid the vicious rum-runner, there was still some chance I'd survive the day. And Aggie, too, of course.

But once the huge craft hove into view, I saw it was not Bonnet, but the Amazons! *The Midnight Sun* swooped down over the cove and began bombarding La Baza's boats with goo. As it hardened, a large number of his men became entombed in it—like those ancient ants in amber. A horrible death, but I somehow doubt any tears were shed for them. (The ruffians, I mean. Whether the ants' friends could or would shed tears is a question best left to entomologists.)

A war party began descending from the Amazon ship via long ropes. I didn't recognize Sesbania among them, but of course I'd never seen her in her pirate-girl regalia. Liz Rutledge had been unrecognizable in hers.

Clarisse tried desperately to dissuade her own ruffians from entering the fray. Once they'd smelled blood, however, they took on the nature of a ravenous school of sharks, giving out a war cry from Hell, then falling upon the Amazons en masse. Cutlasses flashed in the midday sun. Had I not been shackled, I would certainly have raced to my former supposed wife's aid—though I'd have felt a damned fool if she hadn't attended the melee. Which would have been just like her....

With Clarisse's men distracted, and the auctioneer hiding somewhere in the bush, Aggie pulled out her razor.

"Hand over the keys, ya pirate-port bawd!" she ordered Clarisse.

Not quite the insult she might have intended, but enough to draw the bawd's ire. She had a blade of her own, and now the two women circled each other, heaving insults and invectives, but both seeming reluctant to risk a frontal assault.

It was then I caught a glimpse of a white robe flying through the brush. Then another. Then suddenly, they were all about. Nymphs—dozens of them. They quickly disarmed both women, then began tying them up. One of them found the keys on Clarisse and released me from my chains.

"Come, brother-in-law, we must move quickly."

"My thoughts exactly—but that smaller specimen there was actually coming to my aid, and if it wouldn't be too much of an inconvenience, I'd like to bring her along.

Otherwise, they're likely to treat her rather badly."

"Father won't be pleased," the apparent dryad-in-chief said.

"He doesn't need to know," one of her sisters told her.

"Well, all right."

They took us toward the far side of the island, where a smallish airship awaited. This wasn't Bonnet's main ship, but the one he used as a launch, *Le Pélican Volant.* However, he himself seemed not to be aboard.

"Your father didn't come along?" I asked.

"No, he's been rather busy," the number one told me.

"Oh, tell him the truth! Father did some calculating and determined you weren't worth more than fifty-three hundred pieces of eight."

"Fifty-three hundred?"

"Fifty-three hundred and eleven. Father prides himself on his valuations."

"We came on our own initiative," a perky little naiad interjected.

I suspected Bonnet would be insisting I take on a few more wives, and I made a mental note to add her to my shopping list.

"What do we do with *her?*" one of them asked, pointing to Aggie.

"She'll have to become one of us."

"Wrap myself up in a sheet? Not on yer life, sister."

"Well, either that or become a scullery maid in the kitchen."

"Scullery maid?" There were times when Aggie shed the affected vernacular, and this was one of them. Acting the girl from the tenement lost its allure when it involved slaving like one. "Yeah, all right. I'll wear the sheet."

"How will we explain that *awful* haircut?"

"Well, we'll say she cut it to make Father a bracelet from her locks."

"*Jesus.* I think I'm gonna be sick."

"Oh, Father wouldn't like that. A nymph must always wear a smile."

"*Not this nymph!*"

"Smile, or scrub brush: your choice."

While they took her off for her enrobing, I was shown to the bathhouse. It was smaller than the one Percival had constructed on *Lucy*, but otherwise quite similar. I waited a moment for the two attendants to take their leave, but it quickly became clear they intended to stay. They undressed me with a deftness few others than nymphs could muster. These happened to be naiads, one of them the perky girl I mentioned earlier. Her sister—though not quite so jaunty—was every bit as becoming. She was older, but I doubt more than twenty, twenty-one. She spoke in breathless tones that lent her words a sort of desperation.

"Oh, dearest brother! I can't begin to tell you how we missed you...."

"No," her sister agreed. "But we can *show* you...."

At first, they merely scrubbed my body—thoroughly, but quite gently. Then I felt one of them kissing my back, while the other caressed my feet. Then my ankles. She skipped from there to my thighs. These she gradually coaxed apart—though to be honest, it didn't take much coaxing, and it was anything but gradual.

I had every intention of stopping them before things went too far. But while I was considering how best to achieve that aim, and without giving offense, she was upon me, and doing as I have done to so many—*and* underwater. It was an impressive effort by any measure. She took me to the brink, came up for air, then went down again—and again. Finally I pulled her up. She moved her lips up to my mouth, and I thought it might still be possible to back out of the affair before things went past the point of no return. That was before I realized her older sibling had taken her place below deck. Well, suffice it to say, she made her sister seem a novice.

"It's time, I think," she said, on coming up for air.

"Oh, it's my turn! You *always* get to go first, and it'll be another half an hour before I get mine."

I thought they were alluding to the act itself. But when her sister acquiesced, perky retook her position, head between my thighs. They meant to finish me off with nothing to show for it themselves.

"Wait, let me repay you, kindness for kindness."

The perky one giggled. "But we have no... you know."

Well, I've met plenty of women ignorant of their own anatomy, but who would have expected nymphs to number among them?

I started on the senior of the two. As is so often the case with women who speak in breathless tones and sounds of desperation, she had an itch just aching to be scratched. And scratch I did. She paged Zeus, then Hera, Apollo, Athena, Aphrodite, Ceres—the whole Greek pantheon. I brought her through the demigods, all the way to the minor characters of the *Iliad*. At Chryseis, she let out a moan to wake the gods—then collapsed.

Her sister was looking on in amazement.

"Is she... *dead?*"

"No, just deservedly content."

Unsure if she believed me, she leaned down and placed an ear to the woman's mouth. On noticing her, her sister smiled.

"Can you do the same to me?"

"Well, I can give it the old college try."

And I did.

She didn't call on the gods, just giggled. But hers was a giggle with plenty of variation. She ran up and down the scale, sometimes in a pitch so high it could crack crystal, and sometimes in one so low it seemed impossible it originated with this elfin female. Simultaneously, the rhythm varied as well. All very curious. Speaking personally, however, I haven't much use for a syncopated giggle you can cut glass with. It might have been enough for me to lose interest in the endeavor—had her older sister not slipped below and started back in on me. Just as I exploded, perky let loose a giggle that quite nearly cracked my skull.

CHAPTER 3.

THE MOLLY MAGUIRES, REBORN

The three of us were still entwined, all thoroughly exhausted, when there came a knock on the door. The girls slipped on their robes and were preparing to make their exit when Aggie let herself in.

There is one thing to be said for aquatic sex: the bodily fluids which so often give one away are diluted beyond recognition. Regrettably, there was plenty else to arouse Aggie's suspicion. First, the mosaic floor was covered in water, a testament to the energy expended. Second, the robes, having been donned before the playful naiads could towel off, were damp, and therefore translucent. Third, the perky nymph—now looking something well short of perky—found it necessary to lead her weary sister by the arm. Aggie watched them make their way out, then turned slowly to face me.

She'd been done up in the requisite nymph costume: sandaled feet and a flowing robe clasped by a glass brooch. Since they normally wore their hair long and gently knotted, and she hers in a sloppy bob, the nymphs had simply settled on rendering it more classically stylish. Black shiny beads had been woven into her like-colored locks, and her bangs cut perfectly straight across her forehead. Cleopatra gone flapper, I'd call it.

"I must say, Aggie, the look becomes you."

"Save it, skeezicks.... I should've known.... First chance you got."

"Look, you don't know the facts, Aggie. Smedley's been having his way with these nymphs. They just presumed.... Before I knew what was happening, they were upon me. I had to play the part. And... well, after all, I'm only human."

"If that...."

"I won't let it happen again, Aggie. Next time I'll be on my guard."

"You're damn right it won't happen again!" She tossed me a towel. "Hey, wait a minute. If he's been having his way with these nymphs, why aren't there a slew of little nymphs and satyrs—or whatever ya call a he-nymph—running about the place?"

"I was being imprecise. I should have said, he was having them have their way with him. Or maybe it should be, have his way with him...."

"*Jesus.* Yer soundin' like a lawyer again."

"He somehow trained them to... service him selflessly."

"You mean, he got them to... pay the piper—and with them gettin' *nothin'* in return?"

"Well, I never heard that particular locution before. But if pay the piper means what I think it means, then, yes."

"That's 'cause you never met my junior-year roommate...."

"Popular girl, I imagine."

"Yeah. Never had a bit of trouble gettin' a date. 'Course, nymphs don't date."

"True. But they're hereditarily inclined to please."

"Well, I ain't lettin' no one put the boots to me who's havin' 'em licked clean by a sorority house of flautists. Got it?"

"Of course, Aggie. But how do I stop them from... presuming?"

"Easy. Tell 'em you got the clap."

"A little brutal, isn't it? And what if they don't believe it?"

"Already do—all except those two givin' you the panpipe concert in here."

"You've been spreading rumors about me?"

"Yeah. I knew you wouldn't be able to keep your meat hooks off of 'em. And I figured you'd prefer my rumor-spreadin' to castration. But feel free to correct me if I'm wrong."

"No, no.... Were they shocked?"

"Didn't know what it was. Thought I was makin' it up. But when I described the oozin' blisters, an' how their noses would be fallin' off, they got to believin' pretty quick."

"Going noseless would certainly put a damper on a nymph's prospects."

When we dined that evening, I was placed at the head of the table, with Aggie on my left, and the next three places vacant on both sides. We served ourselves from separate platters and were given our own carafe of wine. Our hostesses weren't openly hostile, just determined to remain uncontaminated.

The two naiads I'd dallied with earlier were there, and apparently their sisters had imparted Aggie's revelation. The older one just sat staring at the plate before her. A despairing nymph is a sad sight indeed. Her once-perky sister was similarly preoccupied. Every minute or so, she'd pick up a little hand mirror to make sure her nose was still in place.

The social ostracism was difficult, but at least Aggie wasn't so vindictive as to withhold her affections—just so long as I showered her with a constant flow of devotion and showed not the slightest hint of noncompliance with her directives. The next day at lunch, my eyes fell briefly upon an arresting oceanid (one of those rare women who can sport a tiara of kelp and have it look smart). Half a second later, my sleeve was pinned to the table by a serving fork.

As we left the meal, Pitys, the dryad-in-chief, handed me a note. Actually, she handed it to Aggie for her to give to me. Once we were in our cabin, she read it.

"She says we'll be meeting up with Bonnet tonight. An' she ain't sure how he'll take to you bunkin' up with yer mistress, i.e., me. She's also worried about your wife's nose.... Who's she talkin' about?"

"Smedley's married to one of the Graces. Euphrosyne, I think it is."

"What's she look like?"

"Oh, kind of frumpy. And a very dull conversationalist. But Smedley said she's pretty easy-going. And we just need to tell Bonnet we're married. Adultery may be a sin, but bigamy is downright encouraged."

"All right. We tell *him* that—but don't go thinkin' you got me tied up."

"Heaven forfend."

"Whattaya mean by that?"

I've never walked on literal eggshells. But honestly, it couldn't be any more precarious than navigating Aggie's various moods that trip. She'd never been an easy woman to read, not like Clem. Or even my wives, the Mortal Sins. Sure, they had their faults—but one never needed to guess what was motivating them. For instance, Avarice would have happily slit my throat for a quarter-ounce of gold dust, whether the offer was made today, tomorrow, or a week from Thursday.

Aggie was the polar opposite. One minute she found the mere idea of being attached to me thoroughly repugnant. But a moment later, all that mattered was that she have an exclusive claim.

We rendezvoused with Bonnet over the Smoky Mountains. The mad pirate greeted me like a long-lost son. Apparently, he felt some genuine affection for Smedley—not ten thousand pieces of eight worth, but some.

I was still looking convincingly gaunt from my time in jail, so I made use of my imprisonment to explain any inconsistencies he noticed. I won't say he welcomed Aggie with open arms, but he did accept my story that we'd been married in Tortuga. When he insisted on speaking with her alone, however, I did everything I could to avoid it. Aggie'd made her views on polygamy quite clear and I worried the conversation might veer onto religious topics. As it turned out, they shared an interest in Elizabethan literature. From then on, Bonnet addressed Aggie as Beatrice. A little charitable, I thought. My first choice would have been the shrew, Kate.

The problem of how to accommodate Euphrosyne, Smedley's wife, was solved with equal ease. The rumor of my affliction reached her soon after we boarded. As one might expect, she handled the situation most graciously. Instead of embarrassing me publicly, she let it be known she herself was suffering from some vague ailment that required she remain in her apartment and forgo her wifely duties.

II

The next day, Bonnet invited me to his cabin for lunch.

"I have a little mission for you."

"Well, you just need to ask. Anything I can do to help.... Just so long as it isn't too taxing—I'm not quite up to snuff."

"That's not what I heard." He wore an arch smile. Had those naiads been talking? "Your room is next to Megaera's. This morning, she lodged a complaint about the noise. I suspected Beatrice was the type to work a man hard!"

"Well..."

"Anyway, in the future, try to keep it a little quieter. The Furies can be a tad difficult. Better not to provoke them."

"No, certainly not. What exactly is her mandate? I seem to have forgotten."

"Punisher of infidelity, broken vows, and theft."

Good God! My own personal Nemesis, bunking in the room beside mine!

"Please tell her, I'm sorry—*deeply* sorry.... For everything."

"You don't need to grovel, just not so much banging on walls. Anyway, I need you to go into New York."

"Sounds delightful."

"It's not for your pleasure. I've been having trouble making collections since you've been gone. Here's a list of those in arrears. You can take the launch down. Meanwhile, I'll be heading up to St. Pierre."

"St. Pierre? An auction?"

"Yes, someone claims to have a palimpsest hiding a lost play of Sophocles."

"I suppose it's unlikely to be a musical comedy."

"Depends what you find funny, I imagine."

I forgot for a moment I was speaking with a pirate.

"You leave in an hour. And remember: don't take no for an answer!"

I made the mistake of suggesting to Aggie it might be safer for her to remain behind.

"Safer for whom? Listen, bimbo, don't think you can sneak off like it's some lodge convention, three days of Sodom and Gomorrah away from the ol' ball an' chain. *This* ball an' chain is comin' along, *see?*"

"Of course. All the better. But just out of curiosity, which lodge is that? Surely not the Odd Fellows?"

We boarded the launch with just a skeleton crew of nymphs, not more than two dozen altogether. They moored the craft along the riverfront, about where the abutment for the Manhattan Bridge would have been if Cousin Emmie had remembered its existence. Once we left the ship, they were to hover over the city until rendezvousing with us in two days' time.

In order that she not stand out in the crowd, or freeze in the winter air, the nymphs had provided Aggie with a stylishly cut wool suit.

"How do I look?" she asked, flashing open the jacket and revealing a sheer silk blouse worn over a skimpy black chemise.

Always a dangerous question with a woman. But in this case, there was no reason for deceit.

"Very smart."

"And?"

"Well, simply stunning. Like night and day compared to the way you were dressed that night we met."

I should have stopped at stunning.

"What was wrong with how I was dressed?"

"Oh, nothing. Nothing at all." I wondered, did she remember she'd been wearing a dead bird on her head? "I just think this fits you better."

We stopped by a speakeasy she frequented back in the real New York for martinis. She ran some names past the bartender, but he knew none of her friends.

"Must be new," she said to me.

"I think you'll find only the geography is similar. People are all different."

"Yeah? Anything else?"

"Well, I've noticed some anachronisms. For instance, I sent a telegram to my cousin in Brooklyn and the reply came from Walt Whitman."

"An' I'm an elephant."

"It's true. If there's time, maybe we can stop by and I'll introduce you."

"Yeah, why not? We can ask him about his pond snipe."

It was odd seeing a New York without the ubiquitous yellow cabs. And the elevated trains were back to running on steam. Most incongruous of all were the fashions. Women's wear ranged all over the map. A girl laced up like an antebellum *grande dame* would be seen strolling beside a matron wearing a skirt that barely covered her behind. That's not to say there were no identifiable fads. The most noticeable was the penchant for affixing metal jewelry to cheeks, noses, and lips. This was practiced by both sexes and all social strata, if with varying degrees of success. Trends come and go, of course, but I have my doubts there will ever be a time when a row of rivets across an otherwise comely girl's cheek is seen as working to positive effect. And what happens next season, when industrial fasteners are passé?

I took some comfort in the fact that the Christmas displays were every bit as gaudy as in real New York. It was just a few days before the holiday and simulated sentiment all but dripped from the lampposts. I considered buying Aggie something to mark the occasion, but before I had the chance, she presented me with a sausage she bought from a street vendor.

"Now you buy me one and we're done with Christmas for this year."

We ate, and laughed—mostly because the sausage was so god-awful. I saw nothing moving in it, but at the next speak we came upon, I suggested we purify our insides with another round of martinis.

The first deadbeat on Bonnet's list managed a hotel called the Forum. It was identical to the Plaza, and like it, located just south of Central Park. Apparently, just as in real New York, drink was as easy to come by in the finest hotel as it was in the lowliest dive. I gave my card to a clerk at the desk and a short time later we were brought to the manager's office. Once we'd introduced ourselves, I brought up the seventy-five cases of Scotch and two hundred of champagne he'd not paid for.

"One doesn't like to pester," I opened. "But it *is* twenty-five thousand dollars we're talking about. And there are expenses that have to be paid."

"Listen, I happen to know he steals the stuff."

"True, true. But there's the *cost* of stealing it, not to mention travel, etc. And as you probably know, my father-in-law has quite a household to feed."

"Surely, that's his choice."

"Oh, let's call it religious conviction.... Regardless,

you took delivery, and the stock must be paid for."

"The stock! If one bottle of that was real Scotch, I'll eat my hat. And that so-called champagne! Even the tourists could tell it was fake."

"Didn't you have a chance to sample it?"

"I trusted him! For five years you're a loyal customer, you come to expect a certain amount of integrity."

"From a pirate?" Aggie asked.

"Well, in times like these, one can't afford to be too judgmental."

"So I suppose you're prepared to return the stock?"

"How can I return it? I had no choice but to serve it. But think of the cost to our reputation!"

After a half hour of brutal negotiation, the cost to the hotel's reputation was computed at $7,842.63. This, plus two nights lodging for Aggie and myself, was subtracted from the amount owed.

"But you pay cash for your meals—and your liquor."

"All right, but it better be the real stuff."

He didn't find my joke the least bit funny—however, he did write out a check. As per instructions, I took this immediately to Bonnet's bank. The manager recognized me as Smedley, but wouldn't advance more than one thousand in cash.

"As I'm sure you're aware, your father-in-law has given *very* strict instructions. He's a careful man with his money."

More careful than with his son-in-law, certainly.

Even in New York, a couple could have an enjoyable stay on a thousand in cash. And particularly in fictional New York, where money went that much further. I suggested we eat at the finest place in town, whatever it was, but Aggie preferred an unassuming hole-in-the-wall that reminded her of a pasta shop in her old neighborhood. On the way in, she bought an evening paper and promptly buried her face in it.

"*Jesus!* Listen ta this:

"*A society of hooligans, calling themselves Molly Maguires, after the Irish rebels of the last century, is wreaking havoc in the Pennsylvania coal fields. Company officials have been assassinated, property destroyed, and jurors threatened. With the local authorities cowed by the gangsters' violence and intimidation, the mine owners have turned to the Pinkerton agency to root the menace from the commonwealth.*

"Christ, that happened fifty years ago!" she added.

"One of the anachronisms I mentioned."

"We gotta get out there."

"We do?"

"Don't ya see, the whole thing was a sham! The miners were just fightin' for the right to live a normal life. The goddamn Pinkertons spread all those lies!"

"It's funny, but my cousin's husband takes the same position."

"What's funny about it?"

"Well, he always was a little off-kilter. When I was a kid I lived with my aunt. Whenever he and my cousin came for a visit, he'd offer me bribes to run away from home."

"Yeah? Well, I doubt many people would blame him.... Think a' the story I'd get outta this! I'd damn sure get my Pulitzer—or whatever the hell they call it here."

It's strange how you think you know a person, their whims and whatnot. Then one day, they suggest you chuck your comfortable position as faux son-in-law to a mad pirate and head off for the coal pits of Pennsylvania to do battle with the hired thugs of ruthless mine owners. Not wanting a public scene, I told her I'd think on it.

As we lay in bed that night, after a somewhat restrained bit of lovemaking, Aggie posed a question.

"Hey. Remember back in Tortuga, when Horatio told us the plan of me goin' off to Port Royal?"

"Sure. I insisted you not go."

"Yeah—but you'd figured out that's what I wanted ya ta say, didn't you? *An' be honest.*"

"Well…"

"What gave it away?"

"For one thing, you asked for two thousand, but never clarified in which currency. It was an oversight no truly mercenary woman would make."

"Maybe not the Sin of Avarice, but what about your supposed wife?"

"Sesbania?"

"Yeah, your first supposed wife."

"Not on your life. She has a keen appreciation for monetary precision."

"So you kinda deserved each other."

She'd turned away from me before speaking and I made no reply. I've always found it advisable to allow a woman in a peevish mood to sleep it off.

III

That I awoke the next morning alone in bed didn't surprise me. Nor was I overly concerned when I saw that Aggie had gone out. A brisk walk, I thought, would do her good. When I realized, however, that she'd taken all but seventeen dollars of our combined bankroll, I issued an oath. Then several more in quick succession.

I began dressing as quickly as I could. There, on the bureau, was a note:

Sorry, Skeezicks, but I ain't the girl for you. I'm catching an early express west, so there's no use trying to be gallant and follow me—and no reason to feel guilty for not wanting to. We had some laughs, didn't we?

See you in the funny papers,

Aggie

I admit my feelings were mixed. I already missed her company. Just not the constant reminders that in her book I'd always fall short. She'd tried not to care; it just never really took. Well, *c'est la guerre.*

Just one thing continued to trouble me: yes, the money. I didn't begrudge her a share, but why take nearly all of it? The only answer I could come up with was that she wanted to prove she *could* be mercenary, after all. However, that raised another question: was this another test? Did she, in her heart of hearts, *want* me to follow her? My soul was torn—albeit briefly. Intentionally or not, she hadn't left me enough to travel on. So long, sweet Sheba.

My first appointment of the morning was with the manager of a hotel downtown. It was a swanky, smallish place called the Brittany. I'd telephoned the afternoon before, so was somewhat annoyed when the clerk at the desk informed me the manager was not in his office.

"He asked me to tell you that he needed to check something up on the roof garden. And that it could be some time. He suggested you might want to meet him up there."

I only wish I'd thought to ask what needed doing on the roof garden in the middle of winter, or paid more attention at the time to the clerk's manner. He was nervous, almost furtive. One generally doesn't find nervous, almost furtive clerks manning the desks of swanky hotels.

The elevator operator behaved rather curiously as well. He wasn't nervous, but seemed inexplicably amused by something. When we reached the little penthouse, he pointed to a door. Then he wished me luck. I found this equally inexplicable, but only until I exited onto the roof itself and the first arrow passed within a hair's breadth of my right ear.

I dropped to the deck, then crawled behind a giant pot which probably held a palm when it wasn't twenty-five degrees out. My fall had been broken by three inches of slushy snow covering the roof and this was now seeping through my overcoat.

"Come on out, you bastard!"

"Listen, if this is about any shortcomings in the liquor, I think we can come to an understanding without resorting to violence."

"Shortcomings! It's about my wife, you two-bit Lothario."

"Look, you've obviously mistaken me for someone else."

I started to get up, but the next arrow actually winged my left ear. I could see him now. He was over behind another giant pot, holding a crossbow. For the next half hour or so, I tried to reason with the fellow while he tried to make Swiss cheese of my skull. He came the closer to succeeding. However, eventually his quiver ran dry.

I rose and began walking toward him when he quite unexpectedly produced a reserve quiver. Odds were, this wily hotelier had hunted human prey before. I quickly made an about-face and leapt through the door of the penthouse. I arrived in time to see the same operator close the doors of the elevator. I can still hear his sinister laugh reverberating through the shaft.

A staircase opened there as well and I charged down three or four flights, until I was stopped by a woman.

"You came for me! I knew you would!"

"Well..."

"He's hurt you! Your ear's bleeding."

"Just grazed."

I would have simply run around her, but she'd attached herself like a limpet. Then she licked the blood from my ear and I became weak in the knees. This was a woman who knew how to lick an ear.

Suddenly, we heard someone descending.

"Come, I have a room where we can hide."

She led me out of the stairwell and down a hall. When we came to a corner, she motioned for me to stop. She peered ahead, then pulled me along by the hand. There was a linen cart outside a room where the maid was making the bed. We crept by this to a room for which my escort had a key.

That she was the manager's wife had been obvious from our first meeting. Likewise, the fact that she and Smedley were on intimate terms. But only now did it become clear just *how* intimate—within seconds of closing the door, she had me stripped naked. Not wanting to appear rude, I followed suit.

Well, one can only compliment that manager's taste in women. She was a tall blonde, well-proportioned, and—not incidentally—in heat. She acted as if she'd been given a double dose of the motivating perfume. We stood there, just groping one another with enthusiasm, until she pushed me onto the bed and fell upon her knees.

Apparently Smedley had trained her in paying the piper as well, because she was every bit as practiced at it as those naiads I'd met earlier. She brought me to the brink, thrice over, then we switched positions and I went to work on her. I think it might have been a first for her, but she most definitely did not need any anatomy lessons. Nor did I have any trouble making the acquaintance of her little man in the boat. Primarily because he was anything but little. He was a veritable giant as little men in the boat go.

I think I mentioned before my theory that the sensitivity of a woman's nipples is inversely proportional to the size of her breasts. I'd not assembled enough data to make a similar determination regarding women's boatmen, mainly because the variations in size seemed not as marked. But if this female was any indication, it works quite the opposite. The moment I came within an inch of her bountiful appendage, she began shivering. Then sort of yelping. And finally, emitting something along the lines of a yodel. I have no idea if she held Alpine blood, and it seemed an inopportune time to ask. So I just kept at it until she pulled me up onto the bed. I thought she wanted to finish things off in the traditional manner, but instead she sidled up atop me and then positioned herself bow to stern, as it were. It took me a moment to realize what she had in mind, but soon we were each doing our duty for the other. It's a difficult position, and I'd never had much success with it before. I think it worked with her because the key to her soul was impossible to miss no matter what the angle of approach.

We ended quite thoroughly exhausted, and she fell sound asleep nestled in my arms. Frankly, if it wasn't for her homicidal husband, I would have given serious consideration to eloping with her. But sooner or later, even a bad archer may hit his mark. I slid out from under her and dressed as quietly as possible.

I snuck down a back stairwell, and from there through a pantry into an alley. It was only just after five, but the sun had set and I easily buried myself in the crowd. Back in my room at the Forum, I bathed and enjoyed a pleasant supper of lamb chops, asparagus, and three bowls of sherbet—my tongue was by then feeling the effects.

It'd already been a trying day, and I hoped my next appointment would prove not so taxing. This was at a place called the Riviera Casino, which, rather than a legitimate hotel selling liquor on the sly, was an upscale speakeasy renting rooms by the hour. It was located on a pier jutting into the East River just off 122nd Street, about where 34th Street was in real New York. You see, in Emmie's version, the numbers ran from north to south.

I'd been told the manager's name was Bughouse Louie, which I assumed was just a trade name. Men running resorts like his frequently affect a colorful manner. It allows their bourgeois clientele to pretend they're rubbing shoulders with the genuine underworld. Unfortunately, in this instance, that was not the case. Louie was quite undeniably insane.

The factotum who greeted me pointed to a door.

"Boss's in there—*waitin'*. An' he don't like *waitin'*. See?"

"Yes, I believe I get the picture."

I gave a little knock, then as I opened the door, felt something thump against it. Then a second thump. Gingerly, I poked my head into the room. A short fellow with a severely scarred face seemed to have been throwing knives at the door. It occurred to me then that perhaps this was the season in faux New York for the hunting of liquor wholesalers.

"Hello," I said. "Didn't want to keep you waiting. Is it OK to come in?"

"*Get in an' close the door!* Louie don't like people who waste time thinkin'."

Not a promising beginning. I'd met people before who referred to themselves in the third person and we just never seemed to hit it off.

"Well, I just came about that little matter of the outstanding invoice. Hate to bother you, but it *is* three months past due. Perhaps, if it wouldn't be too inconvenient—"

"You sold Louie bogus hooch! Louie don't like that. He don't like it one little bit."

That was the full extent of our conversation. Rather than go on at length, Louie had learned to express his displeasure succinctly. He pressed a button on his desk and a trapdoor opened beneath my feet.

How long I was out, I can't say. But I woke just as I was tossed like a sack of potatoes into a steam launch (nautical, not aerial). I'd been bound with my knees to my chest and my arms pulled to my back. And whoever did the tying must have studied knots under Ahab. It was all I could do to roll out of the way when the next similarly trussed human bundle was thrown into the boat. There must have been a half-dozen of us altogether. We traveled several miles, I believe almost to Sandy Hook. But then stopped some distance from shore.

A fellow on the boat flashed a lantern repeatedly, then came an answer from above—an airship. A line dropped down with several large hooks spaced along it. One after another, we were attached to it, each still bound into something resembling a misshapen ball.

I've always looked forward to new experiences. But being shanghaied from a waterfront saloon is one I could have happily lived without. As soon as we entered the craft, a gruff-looking fellow issued instructions to three gruffer-looking fellows.

I was about to interject with a brief summary of my resume, hoping my diverse service record might qualify me for some less-grueling form of enslavement, when it struck me that the foreman was speaking in French—and that his voice was a familiar one. It belonged to none other than my old friend Geoff l'Indigné.

CHAPTER 4.

SHANGHAIED

I kept my face turned and prayed he hadn't taken a hard look at me. Having escaped his diabolical machinations twice, I suspected a third encounter would surely drive Geoff some distance beyond mere indignation.

As we were led away, he issued a discordant cackle, whether from malicious delight in our predicament or simply a need to clear his throat, one couldn't be sure. But whatever its inspiration, it was *not* the sort of cackle which cheers the shanghaied heart.

There were already nine or ten decrepit unfortunates at the oars when we arrived. One by one, we were led to empty positions and shackled in place. Nothing about the situation could be termed agreeable. But the fact that the bench I'd been shoved onto was still damp with the blood, perspiration, and whatnot of its prior occupant I found particularly worrisome.

Once we were all seated, our escorts let loose a hearty round of cackles and someone snapped a whip just over our heads. Say what you will about pirates, they certainly know how to motivate galley slaves. We rowed for four hours at a stretch, then were allowed a two-minute break and a munificent teaspoon of water. The wretch sitting beside me wore a long gray beard beneath sunken eyes. His lips were cracked and bleeding, and his bowed back carried the marks of floggings both past and recent.

"How long have you been at it, old man?" I whispered.

"Three, four weeks it must be."

His news didn't bring me comfort. Nor did his clarification that he was just thirty-three, and had been speaking only of his current shift. I presented him with an encouraging smile. He tried returning the favor, but in doing so lost one of his few remaining teeth.

I never thought I'd look fondly on my time as offal packer. However, if there's one suitable apprenticeship for galley slave, offal packer is it. You have the back-breaking labor, the foul odors, and the meager rations. The arbitrary floggings were an unpleasant addition, but certainly not unfamiliar to a husband of Mortal Sins. And for Christmas dinner we were served an actual meal, a tasty stew. It reminded me of something our French chefs had prepared aboard *Lucy's Revenge*.

It was about my fourth or fifth day, I'd guess, that one of the henchmen recognized me. I assume we'd met in the Lafittes' dungeon back in Barataria, because before going off, he examined my hands and appeared very disappointed they both had the full complement of digits. He returned a little later with Geoff l'Indigné, who was even more so than usual on this occasion.

It was imperative that I convince my captors that I was Smedley—and as quickly as possible. Not only had I mightily annoyed Geoff, I'd also welshed on a three thousand–dollar debt to his captain, Jean Lafitte—the amount I'd agreed to pay as recompense for having liberated Clem (my former supposed fiancée's doppel-ganger) from his auction house. What's more, I had allowed him to believe I'd given him a consignment of Mortal Sins, when the girls he took away were in fact the Limnads, aquatic nymphs charged with tempting men to their doom.

The problem was that neither Geoff nor his henchmen spoke a word of English. I tried explaining things in my broken French, but was cut short when they shoved a filthy rag halfway down my throat.

"*Au madrier!*"

He'd ordered me taken somewhere, but I was unfamiliar with the term *madrier*. I did, however, find it comforting that the word was not *cachot*, which I'd learned the hard way meant chamber of horrors.

They led me along a passageway. At the end of it was an open hatch, and stretched out from that hatch was a plank. Well, I was crestfallen. I'd rather hoped I'd get through a book without the opportunity of plunging to my certain death. I'd been fortunate so far, twice surviving the experience, but had no interest in testing my luck a third time.

There were several pirates and captives already in attendance, and one poor soul already out on the plank. Geoff shouted at the fellow who appeared to be running the show, and he shouted back. I only caught some of their conversation, but the gist of it was that Geoff wanted for me to go next, and the foreman of the plank insisted I'd have to wait my turn. It seems there were three fellows in line ahead of me.

Things deteriorated rather quickly after that. Pirates have a timeworn method of resolving differences among themselves and it invariably involves some measure of dismemberment. Blades were drawn, and body parts flew, for as soon as Geoff and his antagonist went at it, their respective underlings did as well.

We captives took cover as best we could, and it looked for a moment as if the man out on the plank might be able to exploit the pirates' inattention by venturing back aboard. He made several forays in that direction, but then a detached limb would bop him on the head and he'd suddenly be in danger of losing his balance.

Once the combatants had been reduced to just Geoff and the foreman, those of us in the queue made our way gingerly down the passage. Where we expected to find refuge is an open question, and one rendered moot by the appearance of Captain Jean Lafitte himself.

He decapitated the two men nearest him, but when he came to me, he paused.

"You! Where is my money!"

I had to speak quickly if I wanted to be returned to the relative safety of a galley slave, and I was thankfully able to do so, now that out of sheer terror I'd swallowed my filthy gag. "I think you've all mistaken me for someone else, that miscreant Van Slyke. I'm Smedley, and very glad to meet you."

"You! Then where's the foie gras you promised me!"

Well, out of the frying pan into the fire, apparently. After decapitating the last of the other captives, he pushed me back toward the plank with the tip of his sword. Just as we arrived, Geoff managed to kick his foe out the hatch, sending both him and the fellow who'd been precariously balanced on the plank into the sea below.

"Wait!" I shouted. "You may be interested to learn that my father-in-law has made it known he's willing to ransom me for fifty-three hundred pieces of eight."

"Fifty-three hundred? *That's it?*"

"Fifty-three hundred and eleven, I believe, was the exact figure."

Lafitte stroked his chin, as pirates so frequently do.

"*And* the foie gras?"

"Oh, yes. Just some trouble getting the right sort of goose. But now, naturally, I can expedite it."

"Well... all right."

Geoff protested as well as he could, given that his mouth had been widened by a four-inch gash across his cheek. But Lafitte brushed him aside and led me to his cabin. Having heard rumors about his predilection for male company, I was feeling more trepidation than I might under normal circumstances—not that being held captive by a ruthless cutthroat counts as normal circumstances.

Oh, how I longed for simpler days, shoveling offal and sleeping in a damp cell....

II

"Brandy?" Lafitte offered.

"Please. And if you have a crust of bread about, it wouldn't go amiss."

He poured me a beaker, then shoved the remains of his lunch in my direction. There was only a little of the veal remaining, but quite a few of the potato pancakes.

"Careful with those, they go right to the waistline." He tapped his belly, and, of course, cackled. "So, what kind of goose is it you require for your foie gras?"

"Muscovy."

"*Liar!* The Muscovy is a duck!"

"Ah, perhaps therein lies the problem."

"No! You aren't Smedley at all. *He* at least put up a fight."

"Did he? Well, it was worth a try." Lafitte seemed in no hurry to return me to the plank, so I quickly cleaned the plate of the last few crumbs. "I heard he was an able swordsman. Fought you to a draw, did he?"

"Pish... He held his own—until Geoff clubbed him from behind."

"Not very sporting."

"*We're pirates!* Not schoolboys. When he came to, he groveled, and then promised me two kilos of foie gras."

"If that's the going rate, I feel sure I could come up with a like amount."

"I won't make that mistake twice! From now on, it's pâté on delivery."

"Well, that offer of fifty-three hundred pieces of eight still stands. You see, all that matters is that Bonnet *thinks* I'm Smedley. And I've already convinced him of that. I was in New York doing his dunning when I was shanghaied."

"Then have you dispatched the real Smedley? And how is it you escaped the Amazons?"

"Well, you see, Marpesia only *thought* she was buying me. In fact, she was sent Smedley."

"And hasn't noticed in six months?"

"Possibly. Though it's also possible she *did* notice and tossed him into the sea—or worse. I'm told she has a predisposition against men generally."

"Yes, so I've heard.... I also heard that La Baza is after you."

"Ironically, his irritation originates with that same girl I took from your auction house. Subsequent to that episode, she rather foolishly returned to him. Then when I happened to crash-land on his island, I rescued her a second time."

"Either very gallant, or very stupid."

"Such a fine line between the two."

"I wouldn't know; gallant's not really my line. I leave that to Jack."

"Seen him lately?"

"No, but he seems to have had his fill of damsel rescuing—knock on wood. I had to do a complete remodel after his last visit, you know."

"Well, to be fair, the place really needed it."

"Bah. Lived-in, that's all. By the way, I've heard a rumor *he's* looking for you, too."

"A little misunderstanding. I put his childhood friend on the market, but with purely innocent motives."

"Oh, *I* believe you. But Jack never waits for explanations."

"Could we get back to Bonnet? He's fond of his son-in-law, and as I say, he's convinced I'm Smedley."

"Yes.... But even if I get the fifty-three hundred pieces of eight from Bonnet, you still owe me three thousand dollars for the girl. And you've now missed two payments."

"I can make that up skimming off the top. Bonnet has a very lucrative enterprise. Oh, and sorry about those Limnads. Not my idea. Didn't prove too much trouble, I hope?"

"Well, they tried the siren act, but didn't have much luck—still, they were damnably annoying."

"Yes, I'm sure. What became of them?"

"You know the old prison on the Dry Tortugas?"

"As a matter of fact, I visited it last summer."

"I holed them up there. Told 'em they could have whoever they lure to it. They weren't keen on the idea—they being water nymphs and those keys devoid of fresh water. But I left them a canteen or two."

"Very generous. And how's Emile getting on? Did a wonderful job with those pancakes."

"He's OK. But I let him get a swelled head. Now anytime someone complains about the cuisine, or offers a little advice, it's *chop! chop! chop!* and into the salmagundi. Let me tell you, you have to be awful hungry to swallow Emile's salmagundi."

"Or be one of your galley slaves."

"Haven't heard any complaints."

"Not terribly surprising, really. Tell me, what's the average life expectancy for an ordinary pirate?"

"Oh, forty, fifty years—provided he comes to the trade late in life. As a pirate, six months, a year at most. Luckily, there's a steady supply of disgruntled seamen and starry-eyed shopkeepers. 'Course, lawyers make the best cutthroats—no need to teach 'em how to go for the jugular. But they're prone to filin' grievances, and then...."

"Into the salmagundi?"

"No—lawyers we don't let off so easy.... But enough chitchat. We need to contact Bonnet."

"Last I heard, he was heading up to St. Pierre to bid on a Greek tragedy at one of your auctions. But that was last week."

"Well, he'll definitely be there for tomorrow's. I've got the only complete copy of the *Ichneutae!*"

"Congratulations. What's that?"

"Sophocles' satyr play."

"What's a satyr play? A comedy?"

"A short farce. Ya see, at their festivals, the playwright would present a trilogy of tragedies, then top it off with a satyr play, poking fun at many of the same themes. Full of ribaldry and hard knocks. In this one, the satyrs are sent by Apollo to seek the return of his cows, which were stolen by Hermes. Bonnet won't be able to resist. In the meantime, I'll have to put you to work. We're short of men right now."

"Can't imagine why."

"Yes, sometimes Geoff takes the indignation a little too far.... But he means well."

He banged on a wall and a moment later a huge brute of a pirate entered. He had to lean his head to one side to fit through the door. His arms were the size of fireplugs and his thighs had the girth of full-grown oaks. A crudely cut gunny sack wrapped about his middle constituted his wardrobe.

"Get him a mop and take him to clean up that mess Geoff left," Lafitte told him. Then he turned to me: "If you don't tackle those loose bits of flesh right away, they're impossible to get up."

"Yes, I'm sure. Well, thanks for not killing me."

"Just remember—I'm of a changeable mind."

He shook my hand, and cackled. Then the giant led me upstairs. His name was Sebastian and it turned out he hailed from the same part of Massachusetts I did—his the fictional version, of course. Beyond that, we didn't really hit it off. To be honest, I rarely hit it off with seven-foot ogres. Especially when they have the point of a cutlass pressed against my midsection.

While he supervised, I saw to the clean-up. Lafitte was right about the adhesive properties of gore. You'd think it had been welded in place. I doubt I would ever have gotten it all up if it wasn't for Sebastian's helpful instructions: whenever he felt I'd missed a spot, he'd point at it, make a threatening sort of grunt, and then knock me over like a bowling pin. Not wishing to be added to that day's salmagundi, I attended to his guidance with diligence.

When I finished, sometime the next afternoon, I was led to a cell and allowed a few hours to recuperate. Being chained to the wall with one's feet dangling six inches from the floor doesn't exactly facilitate recuperation, but I was able to grab a few winks until roused by a depressing thought.

Being myself in the midst of the third volume of a trilogy—one full of ribaldry and hard knocks, and involving a quest for the return of a gaggle of females esteemed every bit as highly as Apollo's cattle—I couldn't help but wonder if I was in the antithesis of the Greek theatrical cycle mentioned by Lafitte: three linked satyric farces to be followed by a brief tragedy. Needless to say, I slept no more. Greek tragedies which turn out well for their protagonists are few and far between.

When the ship came to a stop that evening, I surmised we'd arrived in St. Pierre. The same brute who'd brought me to the cell came by and released my shackles. I fell to the floor. But on rising, I realized that the stretch had actually done me some good. I'd had a crick in my back since my third month shoveling offal and this means of subtle torture had obligingly worked it out. I prayed that this was a portent of good things to come.

Fat chance of that. I was brought to a room where a vat of hot water had been prepared. The giant had me strip naked and then pushed me toward the vat. Unsure whether I was being offered a bath or an opportunity to be parboiled, I hesitated. In his customary fashion, my escort steeled my will with a well-placed knock to the head. Into the tub I went.

I was mightily relieved when he tossed me a bar of

soap in lieu of celery, carrot, and onion. And I certainly wouldn't contest that I was in dire need of a bath. But it did strike me as unusually conscientious, even for a pirate as fastidious as Lafitte.

I'd managed to remove the worst of my patina of filth when the man himself came in.

"Have you gotten word to Bonnet?" I asked.

"Yes. But there's been a slight change of plans. Turns out, he's not interested in paying ransom. Says you cost him fifty thousand dollars by makin' a mess of things in New York."

"Not really fair of him. He hasn't heard my side."

"*He's a pirate!* He don't need to be fair!"

"Does that mean it's back to the oars?"

"No, no. I understand you might be worth even more at auction. Why didn't you mention Clarisse's abortive affair down in Tortuga?"

"I'm trying to block it from my memory. Of course, it came to naught. Just a lot of mutual slaughter among the bidders."

"That's because Clarisse is an amateur. The Lafittes know how to run a proper pirate auction!"

"I take it I'm on the docket for this evening's event?"

"No, you'll be going in Tuesday's. Just after the cognac, and before the truffles. Gives me time to advertise. 'Til then, you'll be on preview."

"Well, I suppose I can at least look forward to filling grub. I imagine you'll want to fatten me up?"

"Just enough to keep you alive. No need for extravagance when all the bidders just want the privilege of slitting your throat."

He punctuated his gloomy prognosis with a cackle. Then, not wanting to be left out, the giant cackled. Then

Lafitte cackled a more complex cackle, and the giant echoed that. They went back and forth like this for the better part of an hour, each cackle, and each response, becoming ever more intricate. Had I not been facing certain death in a few days' time, it might have cheered me a little. As it was, it came a little too close to gloating.

III

That night, I was taken to the recently rebuilt auction house and placed in the very same cell I'd found Clem in six months before [Ed. note: see Book One]. There was a wall of bars across an otherwise normal room, for the easy display of wares. She'd been afforded a second, inner room. But that door had since been bricked over. Another difference was that her imprisonment had occurred during the mild days of summer, and mine the dead of winter. If you're looking to book a cell anywhere in northeastern Canada, my advice is: stick to the warmer months.

Most of the attendees from that evening's auction came by to inspect and cackle at me. Including Bonnet.

"Serves you right. Impostor! I'd bid on you myself, just for the pleasure of guttin' you, if you hadn't cost me fifty thousand!"

I pointed out the illogic of his position (if I'd managed to get him his money, he would have had no reason to want to kill me), but he just snarled, then asked what became of Aggie. Or as he called her, Beatrice.

"Off to the coal fields of Pennsylvania to right a lingering wrong."

"Oh. Too bad. I thought she mighta made a good pirate."

"Yes, I don't doubt she would've."

He went off. But soon after, one of his daughters came by and whispered a greeting. It was Pitys, the dryad captain of Bonnet's steam launch.

"We feel rather bad about what's happening."

"Bad enough to help me escape?"

"Oh. I don't see how we could do that.... But we were wondering if you might share your technique with us. The two you were with have described it, and in detail, but we just haven't been able to replicate the effect—try though we might."

"Well, there's only one way to teach my technique, and that's wordlessly."

"Couldn't you give a rough outline?"

"My lips are sealed."

"Your lips are sealed? I don't see how that would work...."

"Speaking metaphorically. I'd like nothing better than to demonstrate—if you could just aid my escape...."

"Oh, if only we could.... Tell me, why is it *your* nose hasn't fallen off?"

"Oh, you mean Aggie's story of my having been infected. All made up. Out of jealousy. Your sisters are all right, aren't they?"

"Yesss. Lisbeth's nose is all red, but it may just be from her poking it all the time to make sure it's still attached."

"Such is the power of suggestion. Say, couldn't you bring a couple dozen of your comely sisters to distract the guards? Then it's just a matter of finding the keys."

"I suppose that *could* work, but..." There was a loud bellow, like a foghorn, emanating from the floor below. "Oh—that's Father looking for me. I must be off. Farewell!"

The next day, Sunday, it was mostly just gawkers coming to see me—the sort of pirate riffraff lacking the wherewithal to bid themselves, but not wanting to miss the opportunity to take in the misery of my plight. About eight o'clock that evening, however, my old friend Captain Esposito came by.

"So, we meet again! How I've longed to see you suffer!"

"I don't see what you've got to be so upset about. All we did was escape your imprisonment."

"And who do you think paid the price for that? Look at me!"

I hadn't wanted to bring it up, but he *was* looking a little worse for the wear. There were black bruises about his face and his left arm was in a bloodstained sling. Even more macabre, his right leg now seemed a good three inches shorter than the left, and his quota of ears had been reduced by one.

"Run into some trouble in Tortuga? I suppose it was that brawl with the Amazons at my rumored auction."

"No! The boss did this. For letting you get away."

"Oh. Is he planning to attend this event?"

"Of course! He wants to draw and quarter you, and then—"

"Let's skip the 'and then' for now, can we? I'd rather keep it a surprise."

"Yes, I'll enjoy seeing your face when the truth is revealed! Assuming you still have a face when the time comes. By the way, the little one. What happened to her?"

"Gone where you'll never find her."

"Too bad. She would have made a good first mate."

He went off trying to cackle, but evidently it was too

painful for him to derive much joy from it.

For the rest of the night, I was left alone with my thoughts—and they were damned unpleasant ones. I'd never witnessed a man being drawn and quartered, but by all accounts, it's something best avoided. A spell of despair fell over me. Or more accurately, yet another spell of despair—at least the fourth since Bughouse Louie pressed the portentous button which ejected me onto this fatal path. I fell to my knees, and prayed to the one Christian God—and just to be safe, a few pagan ones as well—that a savior be sent to rescue me from my (largely) undeserved lot.

Then, a shattering of glass, and who should come through the window of the cell's anteroom but a smartly dressed pirate. Yes, it was none other than you-know-who.

"Jack! Am I glad to see you!"

"What the hell are you doing on your knees? Lose something?"

"Oh, nothing really. Have you dispatched the guards?"

"The two that got in my way."

"One of them probably has the keys."

"Yeah, probably. Can't say I looked."

"Didn't you come to rescue me?"

"What the hell gave you that idea?"

"Well, the dramatic entrance, for one."

"Ah, that goes with the job. You're just lucky I won't be in on the bidding."

"If this involves Eugenia, it's all a misunderstanding. That ad I placed was just meant as a lure. You see, we each for our own reasons wanted to meet up with Marpesia and her entourage."

"Pretty risky way of goin' about it."

"An error of judgment, which you can be sure I deeply regret. Very deeply."

"And how about what happened that night?"

"Which night?"

"The night you spent with Eugenia—which night do ya think?"

"Oh, nothing untoward, Jack. You can ask Eugenia. I'm sure she'll tell you the same story."

"She did. And I think she believed it—then."

"But now she remembers differently?"

"Well, let's say she has a reminder. Anyway, I just wanted to stop by and say you're only gettin' what's comin' to ya."

"You mean, you came all this way just to gloat?"

"I had business in town—and had to check in with Hildegarde, of course."

"The barkeep? Is she among your conquests as well?"

"I wouldn't want her to hear that. Viking girls got feelings, you know." He looked at his watch. "Listen, I gotta run. We've been bleedin' Peoria dry—now it's time to turn on the tap. Well, see ya in the funny papers."

"Aggie gave me that same send-off not two weeks ago."

"Aggie? Where's she now?"

"The coal fields of Pennsylvania, righting long-dead wrongs. In this case, wreaking vengeance on the Pinkertons."

"*Goddamn Pinkertons!* Why didn't you go with her?"

"Couldn't. She took all the money we had. Then next thing I knew, I'd been shanghaied."

"Well, it's happened to the best of us. Really got to go now. Hope you die quick."

"Very kind thought," I told him. But Jack had already gone out the way he'd come in.

I dozed until about noon, or pirate dawn, then woke with a start. An image had come to me in a dream. I'd fallen asleep thinking of Jack's visit, and most particularly, what sort of reminder could have jogged Eugenia's memory in regard to the night we'd spent together. In my dream, she appeared before me, seated on one of those porch gliders, rocking slowly and smiling, her hand resting gently on her distended belly....

I suppose I should have counted myself lucky that Jack hadn't dispatched me on the spot. But at least that would have fulfilled his wish that I die quickly.

It was now just one day before the auction, but being a Monday—the usual day of rest for both pirates and pirate-port auction houses—I was spared the customary parade of gawkers. The sole visitors were the two iron-workers who came to affix bars to the window Jack had crashed through. There was only one other window, on the outer wall of my cell proper—more of a slit, really. If I could enlarge it by removing a course or two of bricks above or below it, I might just slip through. Thankfully, the starvation diet I'd been on for most of the previous six months had left me with the physique of a tape-worm.

The guard who came for my gruel bowl that day was notably inattentive and I managed to secret the metal spoon away. With that, and a good deal of luck, I just might make my escape. I'd already noticed that several of the bricks surrounding the window had turned soft with age.

I had to work carefully during the day, as the guards tended to check in on me every hour or so. But with nightfall, they took to rum. (I don't mean to give the impression they abstained during daylight hours. On the contrary, they drank from the moment they woke until they finally passed out. But once the sun set, it became their lone preoccupation. Well, and cackling, of course.)

Progress was slow, as the wall was a foot and a half thick, so a dozen bricks would need to be removed to gain even a couple inches of opening. And whenever I heard the slightest noise, I froze and waited to be sure I wasn't being noticed. It was during one such episode I heard a distinctive "Pssst."

I hesitated to respond, but given that my certain death was imminent, I thought I could afford to be a little reckless. So I returned the pssst.

"You're supposed to ask, *who's there?*" a familiar voice instructed.

"Is that you, Sesbania?"

"Yes, it's me."

"Come closer so I can see you."

"I can't, it's too high."

"I always hoped we would reunite. I suppose you have something to knock out the guards...."

"No, sorry. But I *have* convinced Marpesia not to bid on you."

"Really? I appreciate the thought, but I'd rather hoped she'd prevail and *then* you could convince her to give me a reprieve. You see, as it stands, I'll fall into the hands of La Baza. And at an insultingly low bid."

"Well, there'd be no chance of a reprieve, believe me. I only convinced her not to bid because you're destined to die a horrible death one way or another, and she may as well save her money."

"True enough. But why does she have it in for me? If it's that ad I placed...."

"It's mostly that. You see, she and this Eugenia... Well, they're friends. Let's leave it like that."

"Much in the same way as you and Marpesia?"

"Oh... Has Antiope said something?"

"Yes, she did drop a few hints."

"Well, I won't make any apologies to you. You've racked up quite a score—seven wives, the make-believe me—*and* that newspaperwoman, *and* that Bahamian dictator, what's-her-name...."

"Gertie. She's tough, but not without a heart."

"Which she displayed by sending that impostor in your place?"

"Well, yes, for instance. By the way, what's become of him?"

"He's still aboard. We've found he has his uses."

"You mean...?"

"I'll say no more. Now perhaps you can tell me, what happened to my replacement?"

"Believe it or not, she's on the other side, pretending to be you."

"She told me that was the plan, but that you would be going with her."

"Well, things didn't work out that way. I left her with Baker."

"*Baker?* How could you?"

"Quite easily. I told her you had a crush on him, and I think that made her predisposed. Then I left her with a handkerchief scented with that perfume Antiope brought aboard. You know the stuff."

"Yes... Well, I suppose for you that counts as a self-less act. Especially since Baker will now be enjoying that inheritance you lusted after."

"I don't remember you showing any willingness to forgo the money by marrying me."

"Oh, recrimination is pointless. I must get back. If Marpesia finds out I came, she'll change her mind, and I couldn't bear to watch you be drawn and quartered."

"Yes, well I'm glad you won't have to watch. I only wish I could miss the show as well."

"Farewell, Pluribus. If only things had turned out differently...."

"They still could," I told her. But she had gone.

No sooner had I returned to my work with the spoon than I remembered the handbill Lafitte had printed to advertise my sale. He'd asked me to check the English-language version for spelling errors. Along the bottom, it read:

All sales final. A 20% buyer's commission applies. In the event there are fewer than two bidders for any lot, said lot may be divided at the discretion of the auctioneer.*

*Single-item lots of antiquities and females not in-cluded.

Were they to start auctioning my digits, every pirate in town would covet a souvenir to hang about his neck. I shivered—partly from the cold winter air, but mostly from this morbid line of thought. However, this was no time to wallow in despair. I steeled myself and redoubled my efforts—perhaps a little too forcefully.

My spoon snapped in two and both halves went fly-ing to the floor.

CHAPTER 5.

NICE WORK IF YOU CAN GET IT

I was on my hands and knees, feeling about in the darkness for the pieces of spoon, when something tossed through the slit of a window hit me square on the head: a set of keys. Salvation!

I held perfectly still for the moment. There were intermittent cackles in the hall beyond, and with the anteroom's only window now barred, I would need to pass that way. I spent this interval wondering who my savior was. Sweet Sesbania was the likeliest candidate, but why wouldn't she have told me her intention? Good ole Jack was another possibility. Maybe he came to realize the hypocrisy of condemning me for what he did with equal abandon. There were also my dear wives to consider, perhaps in town to collect the month's profits from the local Pelican. Any one of them—excepting Sloth, of course—might have charmed the keys from their keeper. Or, in the case of Wrath, simply filleted him.

Once things were quiet again, I began trying keys. The first few didn't even fit the keyhole. But there were more than a dozen on the ring, and soon I found one that fit like a glove. There was a small chance my turning the key would alert the guards, and a near-certain one the noise of the rusty hinged door would. So before taking the next step, I braced myself for a speedy escape.

The key, however, did not turn. Nor did the next one. Nor the one after that, and so on around the ring.

My heart sank, as it is wont to do in such situations. But E. Pluribus Van Slyke is not one to give up easily. (In the interest of veracity, I should stipulate I'm referring narrowly to the giving up of hope in desperate circumstances, and not to capitulation generally.) To make the best of a bad situation, I took the largest of the keys and once more attacked the brickwork around the slit.

This worked about as well as the spoon, i.e., barely at all, so I was afforded ample time to speculate on just who could have played such a cruel joke. Ironically, the same cast of characters came to mind. The always artful Sesbania was forever setting little traps for me to fall into. Nothing amused her more than pulling the rug out from under me just as I thought I was on the brink of triumph. I remember well the summer evening in a quiet corner of a leafy park when I finally got a hand up under her skirt—only to find she'd donned a woolen union suit for the occasion.

And then there was that smug Jack Tigue, setting an impossible-to-emulate standard of chivalric regard and sexual profligacy, and thereby conferring unspoken contempt on any male falling short of it. How I longed to wipe that self-satisfied grin off his face—or better yet, witness some other fellow doing it. As for my wives, specifically the Mortal Sins, cruel jokes were the only sort of jokes they knew.

I worked diligently, but the night had grown down-right frigid and I needed to spend quite a bit of time just blowing on my hands to keep them from turning to ice. I'd made precious little progress when the sun poked over the horizon. That left me just three or four hours until dawn (Pirate Standard Time, i.e., noon) and the next changing of the guard. That first shift of the day was the most dangerous—they not only made an inspection of my cell, they were reasonably sober while doing it. Well, reasonable in pirate terms....

When a light snow began falling, I looked on it favorably. I was just two bricks away from my objective, but it would be a tight fit and the lubricating effect of ice crystals would surely help. Then, as the last brick gave way, the storm began in earnest. A veritable tornado of icy snow lashed against my face. From that point on, I didn't look on it quite so favorably.

I was wearing little more than rags, the remnants of the suit I'd had on when I was shanghaied. But even these were enough to impede my egress. I had to choose: the Scylla of entering a Canadian blizzard stark naked, or the Charybdis of dismemberment at the hands of the Cyclops. I went with Scylla.

Getting my shoulders out would require leading with my left arm and then twisting my upper torso. Miraculously, I was able to achieve this feat. But the going only got more arduous. The resistance from rough edges of masonry was more than a match for the lubricating ice crystals—even with the addition of warm blood seeping from the myriad cuts and abrasions I was inflicting on myself. Were I to offer one bit of advice to others finding themselves in similar circumstances, it would be to get your second hand out *before* your hips. Pressed against your stomach, perhaps. Mine I left trailing down my side, palm against thigh. By alternately twisting and squirming, I eventually reached the point where my wrist met my hip—and there became quite thoroughly stuck.

It was an awkward situation, made all the more so when some sharp-eyed urchin on the street below noticed me projecting from the second-floor window and began offering three ice balls for a nickel. Thankfully, the near-complete lack of visibility and forty-mile-an-hour winds made things rather difficult for the would-be marksmen. There were many near-misses, but only five or six direct hits. I was still recovering from one of these when I felt something quite unexpected at my other end. Someone was tickling my feet.

I won't pretend these efforts elicited a hearty laugh, or even a muted chortle. Given my circumstances, mirth would not come so easily. But I did take some solace that whoever had discovered me was almost certainly not one of my pirate captors. During our few conversations, they'd made it rather clear how they would deal with any attempt at escape. The word salmagundi invariably entered into it.

I could feel hands all about my legs and ankles now. Soft hands, pulling gently. I arranged myself as best I could to aid their efforts, but it was slow going. The hands were moving northward, up my thighs, and one particularly playful one, in between. Not really the time, I thought, but I was in no position to carp. As my head neared the opening, I could hear giggling. Then a slap.

"*Leave it alone, Sabrina!* I won't tell you again."

Then more giggling.

I was still trying to place the voice when I was, at last, freed, and found myself surrounded by what looked like a troop of diminutive Cossacks. They wore great fur coats, and round beaver hats, but chattered like a group of excited schoolgirls. It was the nymphs from Bonnet's steam launch, now dressed for the Canadian winter.

"We've mutinied," Pitys told me. "And we've voted to make you captain—provided..."

"Provided?"

"Well, you have to agree to impart unto us... *you know*...."

It wasn't much of a concession, of course. I rather looked forward to imparting unto them. "You have my word, as an officer and a gentleman." (For what that's worth....) "However, perhaps we could complete the discussion of terms somewhere more comfortable. We'll need to go out the way you came in. How is it you got by the guards?"

"Oh, quite simple: a little soporific in their rum. But let us hurry—it won't last long."

We crept out into the hall, where the guards slept soundly, and then to the auction rooms below.

"You can't go out like that."

"No, I'd prefer not to."

"He can share my coat!"

"Oh, mine's larger! Choose mine!"

"Stop it! That would hardly do. We'll roll him up in that carpet and carry him out."

You might think a group of pint-sized Cossacks carrying a Persian rug across their shoulders in the middle of a snowstorm would provoke attention. But such are the goings-on of a busy pirate port that nary an eye was batted—at least that I could see from my limited perspective inside the carpet.

I don't think you'll consider it hedonistic of me to suggest that I was due for some pampering. Well, from the moment we came aboard *Le Pélican Volant,* I got just that. I was bathed, and caressed; then salved, and caressed; then fed, and caressed. Even asleep I was caressed. Not surprisingly, I had some pretty animated dreams over the next several hours. Then I awoke to find they weren't all of them dreams. At long last, I'd found my true calling.

Pitys requested I visit her cabin at three that afternoon to go over plans. I took it for granted what she really wanted was a demonstration of my prowess at rousing her inner bos'n, so I made a point of eating and speaking little at lunch—leaving the table with my appetite sharp, and my tongue well rested.

She resided in the captain's quarters, but I had no intention of asking her to relinquish them. It was my aim to be as accommodative and gentle as possible with these unsullied maids, for that is what they were. (Technically speaking, at least.)

She was leaning over a large oak table when I entered, busily jotting notes on a map of the Caribbean unfurled before her. Apparently, I'd skipped an inviting rack of lamb for naught.

"I hope you don't see it as a usurpation, but I've been giving a great deal of thought to our prospects, and I've come to one inescapable conclusion. I imagine you've hit upon it yourself."

In truth, my thoughts hadn't veered much from the ministering angels who'd been attending me since boarding. But that probably was not what she was fishing for. "No doubt. However, ladies first...."

"As you wish. It is, simply, that we would have a difficult time acting the part of pirates in the traditional way. This ship is not large, and only lightly armed—and frankly, nymphs aren't the tiniest bit bloodthirsty. There's your swordsmanship, of course...."

"I think perhaps it's only fair to set you straight there. You see, I'm not Smedley. I was merely impersonating him for the sake of expediency."

"Ah. So that explains why you'd never before... you know."

"Yes. I'm that other brother-in-law."

"Then why aren't you with your wives?"

"It's a long story, but the gist of it is that they abandoned me."

"How heartbreaking!"

"Well, to be honest, not very."

"Oh. Were the Sins so difficult?"

"They certainly were a trial."

"I suppose they don't have much choice in the matter."

"No, I suppose not. Anyway, I'm afraid I'm not the swordsman Smedley is—though I do have other talents."

"Oh, so we've all heard. But that only reinforces my point: we'd never make it as pirates."

"Assuming we play by normal pirate rules."

"Precisely my thinking! So I imagine you've already concluded what I have."

I thought I'd reached my conclusion, but apparently not. "Oh, no doubt—but you still have the floor."

"Well, first we need to find out what became of the Limnads. Once we do, we form a syndicate with them, setting them up on some island. Then when they lure the unwary to their doom, we swoop in and make off with the loot! The booty's monetized, we split the profits, and then do it all over again."

"It's uncanny, but those were my very thoughts! What's more, I've already determined where they've been stashed."

"Where?"

"The Dry Tortugas."

"Oh! Splendid. There's something... invigorating

about it.... I mean, sharing such thoughts.... I wonder... I wonder if it extends to..."

It did indeed....

II

I boosted her flawless derriere up on the table, then found myself a low stool to sit on. Pitys leaned back and pulled up her robe. Once I was in position, she draped her legs over my shoulders—and I got down to business.

At first, she uttered a few ohs! Then some longer ahhhs! But eventually, she began chanting paired words in Greek and Latin: *Quassia amara, Pinus cembra, Larix laricina, Acer saccharinum, Acer saccharum, Acer sempervirens, Pinus halepensis, Tsuga canadensis, Picea abies, Abies balsamea, Pinus pinea....*

Some of these sounded vaguely familiar, and the general format definitely so. I might also mention here, there was a fresh, outdoorsy scent about her—not a perfume, something wholly natural—like that of a stand of conifers you've happened upon in the forest. The final clue was also the first: she was a dryad, a nymph of the *woodland*. Once I remembered that, it came to me at once—she'd been reciting the taxonomic names of various trees, predominantly those of the family Pinaceae, the pines and their close cousins.

When she was sated—and I must say, she was not greedy—she slid down from the table and led me to her bedchamber. There we clambered over each other, caressing, kissing, and whatnot, until she pushed me on my back and did to me as no woman had done before. Whether this fell under the job requirements of a dryad-in-chief, I can't say. But I sincerely doubt there's a woman alive—nymph or otherwise—who could match her in determination or creativity. Including her half-sister, Avarice, who had herself demonstrated a similar appreciation for the art.

I hadn't the opportunity to enter her in the normal way, as she'd finished me off so thoroughly. But I sensed that to these girls, that option lay out of bounds. And I wasn't going to jeopardize an otherwise ideal arrangement by pressing the issue.

When all was said and done, we lay in each other's arms, both covered in a moist testament to our amorous workout. Hers, I noted, smelled ever so slightly of turpentine. It isn't an aroma one generally associates with feminine charms, but in the days to come, it worked on me with ever-increasing effect.

There was a private bath in her cabin, and after we'd scrubbed one another down, dried, and dressed, she ordered coffee and took up where she'd left off. (With her planning, I mean.)

"As I'm sure you'll agree, the key is to find a place near a busy trade route where we can situate the Limnads."

"Exactly!" As if the list weren't long enough, there's one more trait shared by nymphs generally that should be added to their virtues: they are supremely naïve. Even Pitys, as bright as any girl you're likely to meet, or man, for that matter, and yet so easily played. It was little wonder they were so often led astray by all those gods and demigods of myth.

"Well, perhaps you've already another spot in mind, but I came up with one here." She was pointing to the Cay Sal Bank, a plateau of the sea floor midway between Florida, Cuba, and the Bahamas. "Elbow Cay. Uninhabited, but for a lighthouse. And that beacon, I expect, we can use to our advantage. Extinguish that, set the Limnads to sirening, and the bounty will come to us, like… like a polymorphic Zeus to a beautiful maiden!"

"Yes. I couldn't have put it better myself."

"What a team we make, don't you think?"

"Absolutely."

"I should tell you, however. The agreement we all came to concerning your… you know… talent."

"Your agreement with your sisters?"

"Yes. It was stipulated quite definitely that there would be no monopolizing. In fairness, and in the interest of harmony, I must insist you spread your favors widely."

"Sure you don't mind?"

"Oh, only a little. The good of the ship must come first. Besides, things rarely turn out well for a nymph who falls too deeply in love. Look at poor Echo, wasted away until all that remained was her reverberating voice. Or Calypso, knocked up twice by Odysseus, then discarded like an old sock. And let us not forget the devoted Oenone, callously abandoned by Paris for fickle Helen."

"Indeed, who *could* forget poor Oenone? Well, since I'm offered little choice in the matter, I will do as you wish."

"For the good of the ship!"

"Oh, yes. Absolutely. For the good of the ship!"

That same evening, we set course for the Dry Tortugas. And then, for the next three days and nights, I worked as never before. There were forty-seven nymphs altogether, and I serviced them all: dryads, oceanids, naiads, oreads, and a matched pair of napaeae. These last were divinities of the glens. Opinion seemed divided as to whether they were true nymphs or some family offshoot. The only differences I detected were the scarlet hair—both above and below—and their insistence we perform a Highland sword dance before (and after) getting down to business.

I was nearly always exhausted, but never hungry. Like a prized racehorse, I was fed and groomed religiously. Though I seriously doubt there's a stallion alive who's had to perform as I did. For the good of the ship, of course.

I expected we'd find the Limnads in dire straits, having been marooned on a waterless key with just two canteens between them. But I had underestimated their powers of entrapment. They'd enslaved a small army of ornithologists, tarpon fishermen, and coastguardsmen. I say army and not navy because strewn about the shore was the wreckage of the craft they'd arrived in.

Pitys advised me to stay aboard ship while she parleyed with her sisters. As an extra measure of safety—to preclude my being distracted by the sirens—she had three of the oreads entertain me with a recital of Sapphic verse. They had the most mellifluous voices, and gave each line so sultry an inflection, any ambiguity in the poet's meaning was vanquished. As were the three of them, in due course.

In fact, our intimate confab went on far longer than the negotiations themselves. It seems that the Limnads' situation was still somewhat precarious. They needed to keep drawing in more victims just to procure provisions. Which in turn increased both their vassalage *and* their need for provisions. All their efforts had done little to improve their fortunes.

I don't know if it's a trait of nymphs generally, or

just those raised by mad pirate captains of the Mormon faith, but all the ones of my acquaintance shared a strong mercantile bent. They weren't greedy, or covetous, like Avarice and some others among my harem. But they did appreciate the common comforts only a reliable income can provide. Not to mention the security conferred by a personal treasury.

It took less than five hours to reach Elbow Cay, and only fifteen minutes to corrupt the isle's lighthouse keeper and sole occupant. This element of the plan was left to me, though its actual execution I delegated to those very bonny lasses the napaeae. The old man had been alone on the desolate cay for some years and seemed quite pleased with the compensation the girls afforded him. And had he avoided his ill-timed misstep during the celebratory sword dance, I believe he might well have survived the entertainment.

"Now comes the difficult part," Pitys told me.

I'd joined her in her cabin for the evening meal.

"Yes," I said vaguely.

"I knew you'd agree! Just as you say, it will call for the most careful preparation."

"Oh, indubitably."

"Yes! The question is, how do we manage to have the Limnads draw the ships off course, but without wrecking them? For if they are wrecked, we're likely to..."

"...to lose their cargoes!"

"Yes! Exactly. And if we lose their cargoes, what's the point?"

"Well, speaking as a man who's been driven to distraction by more than his fair share of femme fatales, I believe there's usually a short period of indecision between the onset of disorientation and the moment of capitulation. Were we to strike from above at this precise juncture, I think the crew might be very easily subdued. Especially if there were three or four naked oceanids splashing in the sea about their ship."

"Oh, excellent! Of course, it will all come down to the timing."

"It usually does. In pirating, and..."

"Yes! *And...*"

Well, I don't suppose I need to tell you how that conversation ended.

III

The next day, we set our plan in motion. We dispatched the Limnads to the lighthouse and then circled overhead seeking likely prey among the many steamships which ply those waters. That night we made our first attempt, on a smallish tramp steamer. I stuffed my ears with cotton and signaled the Limnads via a semaphore lamp, whereupon they doused the lighthouse beacon and took up their song. We watched as the steamer slowed in the water. When it had come to a near-standstill, we began our descent.

Unfortunately, this was a boat of Spanish registry, and the romantic hotheads manning it lost no time in giving up to the sirens. They quickly regained speed and plunged headlong into the reef surrounding the cay. We managed to recover two barrels of sardines and one of anchovies, but these the oceanids devoured before they'd even made it aboard.

Over the next week, we managed two successes, and three near-misses. For our purposes, however, a near-miss was worse than a complete one, as the time and effort could not be recovered. What we soon realized was that we needed to take multiple factors into account when determining the ideal time to strike. Boats that flew the flags of Spain, Cuba, and Italy needed to be boarded within moments of the Limnads setting to work. As did any ship in poor repair—more often than not, lax maintenance goes hand in hand with lax discipline, and lax discipline is the handmaiden of the siren.

With French and American boats, one had a little leeway. And with those flying the Union Jack, one could take a break for a light supper. Whether this comparative resistance had anything to do with Britannia ruling the waves, I can't say. But in this fictional world, an immunity to sirens would be as precious as a ready supply of limes.

By the end of the second week, we'd hit our stride. Things were going swimmingly. We would strip the items of highest value—liquor, primarily—and then sell the boat and what remained of the cargo to a broker who specialized in pirate booty. I was given a triple share of proceeds, Pitys and the six Limnads double shares, and the rest a single share each. Everyone seemed well contented. At least until the end of that week.

It was then that the Limnads struck an attitude. They'd glommed onto the obvious truth they were the only essential players in the whole scheme. First, they insisted that from then on, they'd work only in two three-girl shifts—one night on, one off. Next, they insisted the lighthouse get a complete remodeling. To be fair, it was pretty primitive—little more than a pile of mortared cobbles. Whereas accommodations shipboard were downright luxurious.

Undertaking an endeavor such as this on a wayward

plot of sand was no small task. Getting materials to the cay was problematic, and finding skilled craftsmen willing to make the trip nearly impossible. It usually took the charms of several nymphs, a sleeping draught, and a length of strong rope. Only the recalcitrant cabinetmaker necessitated my resorting to a cudgel. In spite of these challenges, the work was completed in record time, and the Limnads were once more placated.

A mere day later, however, something rather ominous occurred. I was sharing the bathhouse with the same two naiads I had on my first trip aboard *Le Pélican Volant*—Lisbeth and Sabrina, I'd since learned. Until then, I held something of a monopoly on servicing the girls. Oh, they'd caress and kiss one another, but that which is my special talent appeared to be off the table. I'd assumed this was due at least partly to inclination, as it seemed unlikely the thought of it had never occurred to them, especially since Smedley had them doing unto him as he never did unto them. But apparently, that was not the case.

I was working on the older of the two, Sabrina, with the younger attending to me, when Lisbeth abruptly left her station and straddled her sister, facing away from me and her bower of bliss just over Sabrina's pleasing lips. They exchanged no words, nor did they evidently need to. I wasn't sure at first what was going on up there, but I soon realized Sabrina's playful tongue was mimicking each and every movement of my own, for every time I gave Sabrina's little boatman a thorough dunking, Lisbeth (a virtuoso giggler) let forth one of her glass-cutting arrangements. I pulled out all the stops, making things as complex as possible. But Sabrina had learned all my tricks by then and used them to equal effect. There was no winning. When I left the room, they had switched positions and seemed to have forgotten all about me. Well, needless to say, the handwriting was on the wall.

I should have seen it coming, of course. Pitys had stipulated that my end of the bargain included imparting the technique, and that could be taken in two ways: performing *or* instructing. At the time—facing a certain death preceded by a likely dismemberment—the distinction hadn't struck me as important. But I suppose the one inevitably follows the other regardless of one's intentions.

News of Sabrina's breakthrough—along with schematics provided by an oread with a flair for draftsmanship—spread quickly about the ship. By the third day, my orders were being routinely ignored. And when I went to Pitys to complain, she refused to see me. When she *did* finally allow me an audience, it was to dictate terms.

"I don't want you to think we aren't grateful—for we are! It's just that... well, what's the point, really?"

As I had on several occasions before—with her and others among her sisters—I tried explaining the point, i.e., coupling, but the very idea of it disgusted them. I don't think it was the act itself so much as the psychological implications—to couple with a man was for him to take possession. And the prospect of a pregnancy, followed by childbirth, was something to be feared. Invariably, the cautionary tales of Oenone and Calypso entered the conversation.

Nymphs are, as I've noted, chock-full of virtuous traits—but they lack the maternal instinct categorically. Personally, perhaps because I'd never been on the receiving end, I could take or leave the maternal instinct. But the simple truth of it was, they had no further use for me.

"That steamer we captured last night," she continued. "We thought we'd let you take that, wherever you wish!"

"You mean the rusted-out, glorified tug?"

"It's still afloat, isn't it? *And* we're providing you a dozen cases of rum!"

"How about some of that Scotch we took the night before?"

"Oh, I wish I could—honestly! But I'm afraid that's already been promised to a hotelier in Miami."

"Well, can I at least recruit a crew from amongst your charges?"

"You can try, but I don't think you'll have much luck. There are three men still aboard willing to serve with you.... Of course..."

"Of course?"

"Well, the napaeae."

"The nymphs of the glens?"

"So-called. Don't get me wrong—I've nothing against them. They just aren't us, if you know what I mean. Meg and Una can be a little headstrong. And changeable."

"Redheads usually are...."

"Yes. Well, if you'd be willing to take them along, they just might accommodate you. Do you think you could handle them?"

"You forget, I number Pride and Wrath among my wives—redheads and Mortal Sins besides."

"Yes, however do you manage them?"

"The key is not to aim so high. I've survived them, and that's something to be thankful for. But suppose I do take the napaeae off your hands. Will you throw in a half-dozen cases of Scotch?"

"All right. But you better be careful not to let them near it."

As it happened, the napaeae were no more fond of the nymphs than they were of them. They saw themselves as several rungs above their sisters in the pagan hierarchy and resented having to feign an egalitarian spirit. We were to set off the next morning, and spent the night the three of us together. These two still placed some value on my ministrations—though I'll admit my promise to uncork a bottle of Scotch played no small part in coaxing them to my quarters.

Pitys was right to have warned me—the drink affected them greatly. But I can't say I minded. For Meg and Una, Scotch worked in much the same way as *Deux nuits d'excès* did on other women. With dawn, we were de facto man and wife and wife. What's more, I was every bit as sore as the morning after my memorable session with their sisters, Pride and Wrath. What they lacked in callous cruelty, they made up for in rugged Highland stamina.

Best of all, they came in very handy when we boarded *The Sea Ass*. The three crewmen remaining aboard the aptly named bucket of rust—all Haitians—weren't quite as biddable as Pitys had led me to believe. Furthermore, they were large. Very large. All three simply refused to follow my order to weigh anchor. It may be my French was inadequate to the task, but that didn't explain their threatening glares. We were at an impasse.

Observing my predicament, the girls brought out their claymores and broke into their sword dance. The Haitians were struck dumb. Especially the fellow who'd moved in a little too close to the performance. Though I suppose beheaded would be the more accurate term.

There were no threatening glares when I repeated the order to weigh anchor. However, the decapitation of their comrade didn't help much with the remaining two's understanding of my French. We were back at the same impasse we'd faced earlier. Finally, it was Meg who pulled up the anchor. One-handed. Little wonder I was as sore as I was.

My plan was to sail up the Gulf Coast of Florida to Tampa Bay. I figured the liquor might fetch a little more there, and I might even manage to sell the boat as a coaster—about all it was good for. I made no mention of this. But on my setting a course north, the Haitians surmised I was heading for Florida. And they weren't the least bit keen on the idea. Not that I blamed them. Fictional America was every bit as intolerant as its non-fictional counterpart.

Even more disturbing, the price advantage of selling the liquor in Tampa was quickly being rendered a moot point. The Haitians loved their rum as much as the ladies of the glen adored their Scotch. And that wasn't the only thing they shared. By the afternoon of the second day, Una and Meg had taken up with Jacques and Simon. And I don't mean they'd paired off. They formed a sort of consortium, combining interests both commercial and carnal. All very chummy, but once more leaving me without much of a portfolio.

They soon arrived at the same conclusion, and the next morning, I was set ashore on an isolated stretch of beach on the north coast of Cuba.

CHAPTER 6.

COMPLICATING FACTORS

It was a somewhat chilly morning, but sunny, and quite pleasant. Not seeing anyone along the beach to ask directions, I flipped a coin—then set off in the direction opposite that which luck advised. That lady had not served me well of late.

The sand was coarse and made for easy walking. Less than an hour out, I came to a fishing village. There I bought some bread and cheese, and after lunching, negotiated passage on a sloop headed for Havana.

I felt delightfully carefree. I had forty-seven American dollars and twelve British pounds in my pocket. In Havana, I could last a month on that. We arrived at the docks in early evening, and from there I wandered about town until I came to a saloon with an American-sounding name. Cecil's Bar, I think it was. Inside was a motley assortment of expatriates, American and European, plus a handful of Cubans. I had on a smart linen suit Pitys had given me prior to our falling out. Not quite the right season for a linen suit, but these barflies were no slaves to fashion themselves, and my entrance went unnoticed. Or so I thought.

I'd just finished a G&T when a big fellow with a blond beard sidled up and ordered me another.

"Don't recognize me?"

"Ah, no. I can't say I do. But thank you for the drink, just the same."

"Kelso. Bill Kelso."

"Good God."

Bill Kelso had been two years ahead of me at the Academy, and had also flown the motorized blimps. About a month before my routing of the circus elephants [Ed. note: see Book One], his ship had been lost over Galveston. No wreckage had ever turned up, nor had any bodies washed up on shore. All hands were presumed dead.

"I heard about you and your ship," he told me.

"From whom?"

"Oh, word gets around."

"Are there many who've... you know, crossed over?"

"Dozens, certainly—maybe a couple hundred now that those Amazons have started a regular service."

"You know about Marpesia? And their taking the women from the S.S. *Paris* last April?"

"Yes—your wife included."

"Almost-wife."

"Ah. Very noble of you, coming after her."

"Well, we've known each other a long time...."

"*And?*"

"And?"

"Don't tell me there wasn't money involved. I won't believe it."

"Well, I did raise some—to finance the mission, of course."

"Oh, yes. No doubt. How many did you bring over in your ship?"

"My crew? A couple dozen, plus a stowaway. They're scattered about now."

"And then there's Gertie in Nassau...."

"You know Gertie? And about her NC?"

"I know about her, but she doesn't know about me. Mum's the word. I'm working on something a lot bigger than running rum."

"What?"

He nodded toward a dark corner and we took a table there.

"Imagine if you could not only cross over, but time your arrival."

"I don't follow you."

"Suppose I heard last July that a certain South American republic was about to default on their bonds. And until a few months before, no one saw it coming."

"This is back there, in the real world?"

"Yes. Now, suppose—just suppose—on my next trip back, I arrived the previous February."

"Well—supposing it possible—you'd sell those bonds short in a big way."

"Exactly what I did."

"Are you serious?"

"Perfectly."

"Say, one of your victims wouldn't happen to be a fellow named Rutledge?"

"He called it a fire sale, a once-in-a-lifetime opportunity. Bought almost the whole lot."

Kelso laughed. I managed to refrain.

"You know, he shifted blame for his predicament onto me."

"Yes, I heard." He laughed some more.

"Not very fair, really."

"No. But I figured it only made up a little for everything you *did* do and got away with. Besides, you're safely here, aren't you?"

"By the skin of my teeth. So..."

"So?"

"What's the secret?"

"Really, now..."

"Well, how about a hint. Does it involve speed?"

"Not an inordinate amount."

"And what sort of craft are you flying?"

"Oh, just a normal, everyday steam-powered airship—with a few refinements."

"Such as?"

"I'll never tell. But I will share this: the key is to remember that the laws of physics apply here only loosely."

"I've noticed that. And the geography is muddled."

"Yes. It's almost as if we're in a fictionalized world, created by a scientifically challenged mind."

"We are. Didn't you know that?"

"No. What makes you think so?"

"The scientifically challenged mind belongs to my cousin Emmie."

"How curious. You must give me her particulars so I can purchase her books next time I cross over."

"Good luck. They've only been printed privately. She's never actually found a publisher. You may have to go to the source—if you think you can handle that."

"A strange experience?"

"It is when she discusses her literary efforts. Say, I don't suppose you're looking to hire an experienced officer?"

"Is he trustworthy?"

"Hardly a fair question between friends."

"Were we friends?"

"Well, acquaintances. If you had no intention of giving me a berth, why tell me all that?"

"Oh, an urge to boast to someone who'd appreciate the accomplishment. And one little task I thought you could help me with."

"What's that?"

"Rutledge's daughter. I know she crossed over aboard the Amazon ship, and then heard she'd defected to yours. But what happened to her after that?"

"Why?"

"Well, you wouldn't understand. But I feel some remorse concerning her. I thought I'd cut her in on a share."

"Very white of you. She's in Port Royal, married to a steamfitter named Percival. Last I heard, he was updating the plumbing at the governor's mansion."

"Care to come along and introduce me?"

"Sure, why not."

After paying for the drinks, he took me to a nondescript airship moored just on the edge of town. It was no larger than *Lucy's Revenge*, and even once aboard, I could detect nothing which might set it apart. But he insisted a full tour was out of the question.

"It's after seven. Come along to the mess and you can meet the wives and crew."

There I learned his wives *were* his crew: Borea, Eura, Nota, Zephyra, Skira, Thrascia, and Kaikia. Though personifications of the winds—whom I heretofore had seen depicted only as male—they looked to be thoroughly feminine in their parts. And, not surprisingly, they were all daughters of my own father-in-law, the mad pirate Bonnet.

For my money, they were a little too variable—always blowing hot and cold (collectively, anyway). Not nearly as dangerous as the Sins, of course, but difficult just the same. At least, that was my assessment until dessert, when Kaikia objected that her Cherries Jubilee had fewer of the fruits than her sisters' servings and initiated a storm of hailstones. I assume a good portion of Kelso's profits must have gone into glassware.

After dinner, he took me to his study—his refuge, he called it. He closed the door, then jammed a length of rope into the crack along the bottom.

"Fresh air is all well and good, but the incessant howling begins to grate."

I commiserated, telling him about my misfortunes at the hands of their half-sisters.

"Good God. Out on a plank, naked? At six thousand feet? ...But what about the sex?"

"Oh, quite satisfying—if equally dangerous. What about these girls?"

"Well, they have an erotic way of embracing, encapsulating your... well.... And never get winded, ironically. That Kaikia is in a class by herself, the little hellion. Entirely worth the cost of the tableware. Borea, on the other hand... She's the only one who's difficult in that regard."

"A little cold in bed?"

"Oh, not by choice—but how can a north wind help it?"

I told him about the inciting perfume. If anyone could get ahold of the stuff, I assumed he could.

"*Deux nuits d'excès*? Two nights of excess?"

"At the very least, if my experience is any guide."

"Certainly worth a try."

After that, I rehashed my adventures of the previous year—not leaving off the more telling escapades with the Sins.

"Wow. Almost sounds worth the risks."

"Almost."

"Do you expect to join up with them again?"

"Well, who knows? What will be, will be."

He was right about the howling—it took me hours to fall asleep. And once I did, I had some pretty fantastic dreams. I woke when a strong gust slammed shut the door. How it had gotten open, I don't know. But I found myself naked and exhausted. The sheets were blown clean off the bed, and I lay drenched in sweat. What precisely had occurred is anyone's guess. But the next morning at breakfast, Eura gave me a breezy wink over her grapefruit, and Nota kept sending little blasts of sultry air in my direction. I took from their eolian flirting that they had been my visitors, and Nota responsible for my sodden state.

About two the next afternoon, we arrived in Port Royal. While his wives went off shopping, Kelso and I made our way toward the governor's mansion. Liz and Percival had been provided a bungalow by that ruler and I assumed it would be close at hand.

Halfway there, we came upon The Lucky Pelican. This was the franchise Avarice had arranged just a week before we separated the previous summer. It was a full-fledged casino, and business appeared to be booming. Things also seemed to be looking up for the weary pelican. The colorful signage showed the bird seated on a stack of gold coins while attended by three shapely maidservants. The only pirate on hand was a shackled slave who waved a huge frond fan with each cycle of blinking neon.

It was Kelso's idea that we give the place a look. Once inside, he made a beeline for the baccarat table. Never having had much affection for games of chance rigged by someone other than myself, I went instead to the bar. I'd just been served some rum and brandy concoction when I noticed the place's long-legged manageress moving about the room chatting with patrons.

She was a difficult woman to miss—especially wearing a diaphanous skirt slit up both sides nearly to her hips. Her hair was still the color of a ripe peach, but this time it was cut close on the right side and long on the left. It had been the opposite way on our previous meeting. At least, that was my memory. (However, given my mix-up with the bums and moles, I wouldn't have wanted to wager on it.)

When she passed near, I greeted her. She pretended to recall my name, but it wasn't until I reminded her that Avarice was Mrs. Van Slyke that she remembered our meeting.

"Oh, how auspicious, your coming in today."

An odd choice of words, I thought. Had I gained so high a reputation?

"I wonder if we wouldn't be more comfortable in my office?"

"Sounds lovely."

She led me through a beaded curtain, and then into a small room that turned out to be an elevator. Her "office" sat like a sort of penthouse on the roof of the casino, though it more closely resembled one of my wives' suites in their seraglio than a place of work. It was furnished lavishly, to a point just shy of gaudy, and opened onto terraces in all directions, thereby catching even the slightest breeze.

She directed me to a pile of cushions. Once I'd seated myself, she stretched out on another pile beside me. Her facial features, though not otherwise distinguished, were symmetrically perfect, and I wondered if the coiffure wasn't partly to accentuate this fact.

"Why is it we've missed the pleasure of your company for so long?" she asked. "Not since that first visit. You and your wife... You *are* still together?"

Vain as I am, I'd deduced before we'd even passed through the beaded curtain she hoped to wheedle something out of me. And that it must certainly involve my connection to my greedy wife. Some men might be insulted. As for myself, I rather enjoy being wheedled.

"Oh, of course. It's just my work necessitates a good deal of travel."

"Then I imagine you're here to meet up with her tomorrow?"

Don't blow it now, Pluribus. "Yes, the timing worked out perfectly."

"May I confide in you?" she asked breathlessly.

She lay now with elbow bent, her head propped on her hand, her mouth just inches from my own.

"Yes... Yes, of course you can."

"Well, when it came to negotiating terms, your wife, I feel... I hope you won't be offended by my words...."

"Oh, no, not at all."

"Well, she really took advantage of me and my enthusiasm for the project. As I'm sure you know, she takes sixty percent of profits! Now, that's hardly fair, is it?"

"Not the least bit fair...." In truth, it was better terms than I'd ever gotten from the acquisitive Sin. But my hostess's lips were by then brushing my cheek, and her interests and mine had become one and the same.

She pushed me back, and kissed me as I'd never been kissed before. With our mouths still clasped, she pulled my hand through a slit in her blouse and lay it upon her heaving breast. At my touch of her already rigid nipple, she gasped. In a moment, I had her blouse open and was running my lips from nipple to nipple.

"Oh! Oh!" she cried, then buzzed.

Or that's how it seemed. In fact, it was the door that buzzed. And without my realizing it, a retainer had entered. I was still busily working her twin bowsprits when I was startled to hear him speak. Just three syllables, spoken in a very low voice, and I only caught one. A name...

II

Yes, you guessed it. The name was Jack.

"I'm sorry," she said, snapping close her blouse. "But I've a really important engagement."

"Can't it wait ten minutes?"

"No, I'm sorry. I need to prepare myself. He's... He's already on his way up. Do you mind taking the back way? Aloysius will show you."

Well, I didn't have much choice. The last time I'd encountered Jack, he wished me a quick death. Were he to come across me nibbling the chest of one of his paramours, he might be inclined to take matters into his own hands.

The servant led me down a stairway off one of the terraces, and from there out a rear exit. The door was slammed and locked behind me. At least I'd learned Avarice would be arriving on the morrow. Perhaps this would be an opportune time to retake my place aboard *Lucy* and my assorted wives?

I'd need to think on that. My needs would be provided for, but the carefree existence I'd so welcomed the day before would be quite effectively nipped in the bud. I found a semi-respectable tavern and ordered a triple shot of rum. (And I was glad I did. The glass it came in was so filthy it needed that much alcohol just to disinfect it. In a place like Port Royal, semi-respectable means a place from which a patron has an even chance of emerging alive.)

Once equipped for thought, I left the bar and drifted back to where Kelso had moored his craft. There, just three moorings down, I espied Jack's ship, *The Buttered Goose*. Seeing as its captain would likely be away until that night, I considered boarding and saying hello to Celia, an easy-going redhead I'd made the intimate acquaintance of while a guest of Jack's the previous summer. I was still considering the matter, when I saw someone being lowered from the vessel.

I didn't identify her at first, her only notable features being a blonde ponytail and a rounded belly. But once she'd alighted and turned in my direction, I immediately recognized the glum expression pasted upon her face, the little half-moon eyeglasses sliding down her nose, and the shabby suitcase grasped tightly in both hands. It was Eugenia, and she was looking just as miserable as when I'd encountered her in Nassau six months before.

"It's you!" she exclaimed. Her tone betrayed feelings nearer alarm than mere surprise. Whether it included a definite accusation wasn't yet clear.

"Yes, it's me."

"I... I suppose you've come to see Jack. Oh, promise me you won't tell him...."

"Won't tell him what, particularly?"

"That I'm leaving."

"Well, you needn't worry about that. Jack and I aren't on the friendliest of terms. I was just passing by, looking for a friend."

"Oh, good. I wonder…"

"Short of funds again?"

"I am in need of some help."

"Well, I think we can arrange something."

A horrified expression came over her.

"I mean, I'd be glad to lend you what you need. Repayment at your convenience."

"Oh, it's not money I need, just help finding a place to stay the night. But do you mind if we leave the area quickly? Or do you need to wait for your friend?"

"Well, why don't I get you settled somewhere, then I can meet with him."

"Yes—but please, not a hotel. Jack will be looking for me."

"I'm planning on visiting some friends living here. I think maybe I can persuade them to put you up."

"That would be ideal."

I picked up her suitcase and we started walking in the direction of the governor's mansion.

"Maybe we could hire a cab?" she suggested.

"If you mind the walk. But if it's Jack you're worried about, I happen to know he'll be tied up for the next few hours."

"Oh. I don't mind the walk. It feels good to stretch my legs—just so you're sure."

I assured her I was. Two blocks on, I spotted Kelso approaching us. He looked even more miserable than Eugenia.

"She'll never forgive me," he moaned.

"Who? One of the winds?"

"Rutledge's daughter. I'd ten thousand dollars set aside for her."

A memory from our time at the Academy suddenly

flashed before me: Kelso had barely escaped expulsion over an addiction to gaming.

"Any left at all?"

"Six, seven hundred. You take it to her, will you? I'd be too embarrassed, given how much I took the old man for."

There are few circumstances in which I could bring myself to refuse such a heartfelt request. I agreed, then patted him on the back.

"Of course. And don't worry. I'll make up a plausible excuse."

"You were always good at that."

While he trudged back to his ship and his blustery wives, we continued on to our destination.

We'd gone barely ten yards when Eugenia suddenly blurted out, "It's Jack's baby."

It was worded as a statement of fact, but she looked at me now as if awaiting confirmation.

"Yes. Yes, of course it is."

"And we've married, so that's all right."

"Married?"

"Oh, yes. Right here, this morning. I have the certificate."

She stopped and started looking in the leather bag she wore over her shoulder.

"No need for that. Really."

"Oh. No, of course not." She laughed at herself. "I suppose you're wondering why I want to leave Jack. I mean, having just married him. It's rather complicated. Can I just leave it at that for now?"

"Fine with me." Speaking as a complicating factor, I was more than happy to drop the subject.

We'd come upon a street of haberdashers and I

asked if she'd mind my doing some shopping.

"I was marooned with just the clothes I have on."

"You certainly lead an eventful life for someone not a pirate."

"Yes. You see, I intended to stick to the part of privateer, but the lines become blurred rather easily."

"Mmm. That's so true. Many a man has gone to sea with a commission to wreak havoc, only to be hanged later for piracy. The fickleness of fashion."

With Eugenia's advice and prompting, I managed to spend over a hundred dollars in less than an hour. More amazing, the entire trove fit in a single paper parcel.

I made inquiries at the gate to the governor's mansion and was given an address just three blocks away. There we came upon a row of brightly colored bungalows built on a rise overlooking the sea, and before one of them, a woman taking the sun on that warm February afternoon. She was wearing sunglasses and her hair was done up in a tight bun. I wouldn't have recognized her at all except that her belly was even larger than my companion's—about what I'd have calculated based on her report of having been knocked up a little previous to settling down in Port Royal.

"Liz?"

She lifted the sunglasses and squinted at me.

"Oh my God. We heard a rumor you crossed back over.... And then another that you'd been taken by Marpesia...."

"It's a long, sordid story. And one I'll be more than happy to share. But first, I've a favor to ask. Do you think you might be able to put us up? Just for the night?"

"Yes, of course. But aren't you going to introduce me?"

"Oh. Liz, Liz Rutledge, this is Eugenia Biddle."

"Tigue, now," the lady herself corrected. "Eugenia Tigue."

"And I've become Liz Peabody. Odd that the man who conducted the ceremony would forget."

"Pleased to meet you. I wonder, if it isn't too much trouble, if I could have a glass of water? And maybe sit down."

"Certainly."

We followed Liz inside the house, and then she took Eugenia into a bedroom.

"She needs a nap," Liz told me while retrieving a glass of water.

When she returned, she made coffee and we sat in her homey kitchen.

"What are you doing, wandering around with another man's wife in the condition she's in?"

"Oh. Well, I don't really have all the details." And I'd have just as soon forgotten the one detail I did have. "But she married Jack Tigue this morning."

"Really? What an odd pairing."

"It seems they've known each other since childhood."

"Oh, I see. So he allowed himself some liberties with his old friend, and *she's* stuck with the consequences! And now she's torn—she needs a roof over her head and that of her child, but does she really want to live with a bastard who'd do that to her?"

"Yes. Something like that."

"I don't suppose you had anything to do with it?"

"*Me?* What gave you that idea?" She was looking at me skeptically and it seemed best not to give her too much time to consider the question. "By the way, I ran into Noyes Congdon when I passed through Miami last summer. Real Miami, that is."

"Noyes?" She repeated her former fiancé's name with obvious dismay.

The shoe was on the other foot now, but I saw no reason to drive home the point.

"Don't worry. He's engaged to be married, to an old friend of mine. When I told him you'd tied the knot, he insisted on sending along a wedding present."

I took the last five of the hundred-dollar bills Kelso had given me from my wallet.

"He worried you might be insulted."

"Oh, no chance of that." She quickly counted it, then stashed it in a hidden pocket.

"That's what I thought."

"So you've had it for six months and saved it for me?"

"Well, I was honor-bound."

She looked at me skeptically again, but this time it lacked the unspoken opprobrium it'd included a few moments earlier.

"So what are your plans? And hers?"

"Well, tomorrow my wives are expected in town, and I thought I might rejoin them."

"When did you last see them?"

"About a day later than I last saw you."

"But you've been in touch?"

"No, I'm afraid not. I spent most of that time in the Nassau jail and there weren't many opportunities for correspondence. But I'm hoping by my absence, they've grown fonder."

"Fat chance of that."

"Well, at least less dangerous. As far as Eugenia

goes, I'm not sure. If she wants, I'll bring her along."

"You think your wives would agree to that?"

"Only if I can concoct some story that gives them the idea there's money to be gained by befriending the girl."

"Well, if not, we could put her up for a while. Of course, once we start popping out progeny, things will get a little crowded."

We chatted on about this and that, but her primary interest was focused on Kate, Congdon's new fiancée. I gave her all the details I could remember—short of those I'd learned only under the sheets.

III

When Percival arrived home, we had supper. He was friendly enough, but I don't think he was keen on having me as a houseguest.

He'd left for work by the time I rose the next morning, and I sat down at the breakfast table with the two mothers-to-be. At one point, there was a lull in the conversation, which Eugenia broke by informing us she'd decided to go to France.

"France?"

"To have the baby. I have friends there. And I have a French passport. I was born there myself, you know."

"Yes, I remember now."

"You remember?" both she and Liz asked simultaneously.

"I think you mentioned it when last we met." Of course, she hadn't. I'd read it in one of Emmie's books.

"I've heard there's an airship that makes weekly trips between Martinique and Marseilles. I've enough for the ticket. And to get to Martinique—but I wonder if you could arrange that for me? I'm afraid of encountering Jack if I go near the ticket offices."

"Well, if we can get aboard my ship, *Lucy's Revenge*, I should be able to drop you off there. It's due to arrive today, I believe."

"Oh, that would be wonderful. Is there some question as to whether you can get aboard your own ship?"

Liz laughed a laugh three octaves above soprano. In normal conversation, and with some effort, she could generally keep her voice below the threshold of pain. But once she got excited, it quickly rose in pitch well past that point. When she recovered herself, she revealed the broad features of my marital arrangements.

"*Seven wives?*"

"Oh, it's not just the number," Liz continued. "It's who the seven—"

"I think that's enough for now, don't you?" I interrupted.

The girl was antsy enough without knowing that five Mortal Sins counted among my seven wives.

I can't say I was looking forward to a reunion myself. Even my pair of Muses, Clio and Melpomene, had proven themselves troublesome. But after the spell of generosity I'd suffered the evening before—giving Liz the nest egg Kelso had handed me—I was once again broke. If not completely broke, quite nearly so. Soon I'd need to find a job. And the sad thing is, there really aren't a lot of berths open to ne'er-do-wells. There was piracy, of course. But it would be difficult to feign much enthusiasm for an occupation in which the term of office was six months to a year, and ended with a miserable death.

Given all my trials of the last seven months, what I longed for most was the sort of comfort only a stable family life can offer. And it's difficult to imagine a more comfortable arrangement than one where one's wives have a steady source of income with which to support one. Say, a string of lucrative casinos located in shady ports of call.

After bidding farewell to our hostess, Eugenia and I strolled down to a sidewalk café across the boulevard from The Lucky Pelican. There we took a table situated behind some potted camellias. From this vantage point we could monitor the entrance to the casino without risk of Jack discovering his missing wife.

Well, there we waited. And waited. And then waited some more. At the end of the third hour, it occurred to me my greedy wife might have used the rear entrance, through which I'd been ejected the day previous.

"Listen, I have a better idea," I told my erstwhile ward. "Let's find out where the ship is docked and simply board unannounced."

This was surprisingly easy. At least the first part. We took a hansom down to the docks and found *Lucy's Revenge* moored right where Kelso's craft had been the day before—and, rather ominously, *The Buttered Goose* still just down the quay.

The second part of the plan, getting aboard, was quite another matter. I could see that someone had recently been lowered from the ship and I tugged the line to gain the attention of those manning the control room.

"Who goes there!" a loud, forbidding voice called down from on high. I'd never before traded a word with a myrmidon, but I took it on faith that's what I was dealing with.

"It is I, your master!"

"I have no master!"

He confused me with that—I'd always heard myrmidons were rather wedded to an ordered hierarchy. Then I realized he was just puzzled about my position.

"It is I, E. Pluribus Van Slyke, lord of your mistresses, and hence *your* master. I insist you hoist us up at once—or prepare to suffer the consequences."

He made no reply—at least not verbally. But a moment later, I felt distinctly as if I was being relieved upon. As I wiped my face, Eugenia called from the little shed where she'd wisely taken cover.

"Do you need to go through this every time you board?"

"Oh, no. Just breaking in some new staff is all."

"Well, well. Look who's here," a familiar voice broke in.

"Horatio! Am I glad to see you. Are you back aboard *Lucy*?"

"Yes, Clarisse and Mattie didn't get along. And your wives made a nice offer."

"They needed you to run the ship?"

"Me? Just for comic relief, they said. Them myrmidons never crack a smile. It's Mattie they really wanted."

"Her talents as seamstress?"

"Yes. They're bustin' at the seams."

"Ah. That French pastry chef. Well, do you think you can get us aboard? Then maybe we can continue the conversation there. We're a little worried about running into Jack."

"Jack? I heard he's married and not so dangerous anymore."

"Well, this is his wife and she's decided to leave him."

"Oh, well, that *will* make him mad, all right.... The way it works now is, you got to know the password."

"Password?"

"Oh, yeah. Myrmidons are sticklers for regulations. Today's password is Thursday, this bein' a Thursday."

"I see. Sticklers for regulations, but not terribly bright."

Horatio shouted the secret word at the top of his lungs, and a few minutes later we were all safely aboard.

"We're just in time for afternoon coffee," he announced. "Thursday's pastry is raspberry turnover."

He led the way to an ornate dining room, exactly where the crew's mess had been. There, before we'd even sat down, my appetite for family life was quite unequivocally sated. Mattie, the ship's pâtissier, Reynard, and all but one of my harem were seated at the table. For a moment, we looked on one another in silence. A quick survey of the wives, however, made clear that it wasn't pastries, or at least not pastries alone, which necessitated the hiring of a seamstress. Clio, Melpomene, and Wrath were all in much the same state as Eugenia, though perhaps a little further along. (Sloth too had a bit of a belly, but hers looked to be solely due to the pastries.)

It was Wrath who broke the ice. "You! Three months of morning sickness I went through on account of you!" She looked about the table for something to throw, but not wanting to sacrifice the comestibles, the best she could come up with was an easily ducked teaspoon. Normally, she would have gone to the kitchen and fetched a cleaver. So in her case, it might be said that pregnancy became her.

Melpomene, decidedly not. She sighed about how she'd worried her child would grow up without a father. Then sighed because I didn't seem quite so tall as she remembered. Then sighed because gestation had come accompanied by a tendency toward flatulence....

Clio was the only one who seemed genuinely happy about the prospect.

"It's provided a wonderful opportunity to test the hypothesis."

"Test which hypothesis?"

"You know, the power of imagery on the expectant mother. I've been studying Japanese woodcuts assiduously."

"So if your baby arrives Oriental..."

"Mother was telling the truth!"

Pride and Envy were there as well. Envy was, as usual, looking rather frumpy. But when I greeted her with a smile, instead of sending me the customary snide remark, she actually smiled back. Perhaps she was relieved not to be in the same condition as her sisters.

Pride, on the other hand, looked quite unlike her normal self. She had been the most careful dresser of the lot, and possessed of a keen sense of fashion. Today, however, she was looking as slovenly as her sister, and not even remotely prideful. She replied to my greeting with an odd, quizzical look.

I introduced Eugenia, but she seemed rather overwhelmed by the situation. She smiled, and nodded politely, but mainly focused her attention on her pastry.

When she finished, Horatio escorted us to a part of the ship which hadn't existed before. We took a steam elevator to the highest decks of the ship, space which had formerly been a hold. *Lucy* had been thoroughly remodeled and there was little that remained of her former self. Each of the suites he presented us included a personal bath and balcony.

Needless to say, I was seeing arguments both pro

and con for resuming my dual position of titular captain and polygamist husband. Conditions aboard *Lucy* were unquestionably superior to what they had been. On the other hand, while the *idea* of fatherhood had generally appealed to me, I'd always pictured its practical application at some distance in the future. And any expansion of family happening in a measured, sequential way, and not in parallel.

I was still soaking in my quite comfortable bath when a myrmidon named Achilles came by with my evening sherry on a tray.

"Ah, wonderful idea. Thank you."

"You're very welcome, sir."

"It's funny. I heard you came from Greece, but I don't detect an accent."

"I personally spent some time in the employ of an American buggy-whip magnate."

"Ah. Until his business soured?"

"Soured? Not that I'm aware of. No, I simply couldn't abide his wife. A real Xanthippe."

"And yet you get along with the five Mortal Sins?"

"Well, they may at times be trying, but there's no denying they're exceptionally predictable."

"Yes, they are that. I suppose Avarice is out collecting from her franchisee?"

"Lady Avarice has since returned."

"Lady Avarice?"

"It was a bit of a conundrum, just how we were to refer to your wives. Not Miss Avarice, etc. And they couldn't *all* be Mrs. Van Slyke."

"Would make for confusion, I suppose."

"Yes. As I was saying, Lady Avarice would like to see you in her quarters before dinner."

"Ah—where *are* her quarters?"

"Once I've helped you to dress, I will take you there myself."

"Lovely. Say, Lady Avarice... is she..."

"Knocked up? Yes, I'm afraid she is, sir."

"Ah. Not happy about it?"

"Let us say, not ecstatic about it."

"Well, let's hope she's in a forgiving mood."

From the expression he evinced, I took it he knew as well as I did that possibility was a slim one.

CHAPTER 7.

HUSBANDLY DUTY

Avarice's quarters appeared the antithesis of her lodgings in the seraglio: bright and airy, painted all in pastels, and noticeably free of foul-smelling tobacco and incense. The plates and bowls which had borne chocolates and sweetmeats were filled now with fresh fruit and nuts. The main room was at the very stern of the ship and had windows on three sides. As the last rays of sun streamed in from the west, the sheer curtains fluttered in an evening breeze.

I heard her before I could see her. She was in her bedchamber, counting. I assumed it involved her treasury, but when I peeked in the door, I could see she was doing knee bends.

"You'll need to learn to knock," she said. "We have doors now."

"Sorry. You're looking quite fit."

"Was that meant to be funny?"

"No, no. I mean it. There's a... a sort of glow to you now."

"*Oh, please!*"

She ceased her exercising and joined me in the outer room. She wore a diaphanous sort of three-quarter robe gathered at the waist and partially concealing a pair of thigh-length elasticized shorts—what the smart pregnant Sin was wearing that season, apparently. She walked past a couch and sat down in a straight-backed wooden chair, then began lifting her legs, first one, then the other....

"Are you looking to remain with us?" she asked.

"Well, when I heard of... events, I thought I should assume my responsibilities."

She made a disparaging noise, one I didn't recognize—though perhaps her prenatal bulk had only altered a familiar one's resonance. "You're broke, aren't you?"

"Well... It's been a trying period—what with my time in jail, and then a stretch as one of Lafitte's galley slaves."

"Really?" She laughed. "I hadn't heard about that. I bet you made a miserable slave."

"I was miserable, yes."

"Tell me, how can I be sure you're my husband, and not Smedley? It's been so long since I've seen either of you, and so many people have been fooled already."

"I can think of one way.... If you aren't incapacitated...."

"Are you propositioning me?"

"Can you proposition your wife?"

"Don't be facetious—it's tiresome. I've an idea...."

Her idea was to test my recollection of the most humiliating episodes of our time together. She took particular joy in having me recount the details of the occasion when she and her sisters had me out on the plank.

"And what was it you were wearing?"

"Let's see.... Nothing, I think it was."

"That's right. Wrath feared clothing might lessen the effect of the horsewhip she was wielding...."

Then there was the episode where I mistook Clem for her doppelganger, my former supposed wife Sesbania.

"How many days was it before you realized your mistake?"

"I don't remember precisely.... Only until those Amazons boarded."

"You know, I heard later how you offered to hand us over to them. Some lord and protector you are."

"Well..."

"Please, not another 'Well.' There are other ways of beginning a sentence, you know." She was on the floor now, lying on her back and pedaling an invisible bicycle. "All right, you may stay. But I warn you, if you do stay, you'll have your work cut out for you."

"Anything I can do as an experienced officer."

"Oh, you misunderstand me. It's Pride and Envy."

"What about them?"

"They want in on the act." She nodded toward her tummy. "You know what those two are like."

"Of course. I'll do whatever's necessary to maintain the harmony of the family."

"Yes. I was sure you would. But keep in mind, they are both pig-headed women, and their cycles are very closely synchronized—and Sloth's too. She'll probably want one as well. I've ordered you an extra round of oysters with dinner."

"That should help. I suppose you know about Eugenia?"

"Yes, I heard about her. Is she off the cuff, or did you marry her as well?"

"She's Jack Tigue's wife. And it's his child."

"Then why is she here?"

"I'm not really sure. She's determined to go to France to have her baby. Asked if we could drop her off in Martinique, where she can hop an airship to Marseilles."

"All right. I'm planning to go back down to Port of Spain and have it out with that Myra. She still hasn't fallen in line. We can drop her off on the way. But first we need to stop in Tortuga."

"Tortuga?"

"Yes, Tortuga. What's so surprising about that?"

"It's just that I had a rather unpleasant experience there a couple months back."

"It's a fetid pirate port—I can't imagine having anything *but* an unpleasant experience there."

"And yet *you've* never been placed on the auction block."

"Auction block?" She laughed. At first, I thought it a laugh of incredulity, but then it became obvious she simply found the image amusing.

"I made the mistake of asking Clarisse for sanctuary."

"Your time in prison must have softened your head. Well, come along. Dinner is served promptly on the hour."

The meal went off rather well, I thought. Eugenia, seemingly rejuvenated, had a long conversation with Clio about medieval Latin literature. Pride, too, looked restored. She was wearing a revealing robe which showed to advantage both legs and cleavage, and her auburn hair once more trimmed into a comely bob. She spoke hardly at all, but the hungry gaze she cast my way left little doubt about her line of thinking.

Nor did the wet kiss Envy planted on me between the bisque and salad—catching a drip, she explained. She wasn't dressed any differently, but there was an aspect of accessibility about her that would have been hard to miss. Especially after she placed my hand between her parted thighs and snapped them shut.

"My temperature is up half a degree centigrade," she whispered.

"I daresay mine's up at least that much."

"I mean, I'm at my most receptive."

My hand had come to much the same conclusion. Before dessert was even served, she insisted she needed my help with something in her cabin. No one at the table was fooled about her intentions, and particularly not Pride. One hears reports of women looking daggers. But until I married the Sins, I'd never fully appreciated a glare's potential to inflict pain, or at least give a pledge of its imminence.

Envy's apartment was similar in size to Avarice's, but not nearly so neat. Discarded clothing lay where it fell, on chairs, sofa, and floor, and every inch of table surface was cluttered with dirty coffee cups, wine glasses, and dessert plates. In the middle of the floor sat a mounded jumble of pillows, vaguely resembling a pyramid.

"Forgive the mess. The myrmidons are supposed to provide service, but I'll not trust anyone with my things who was hired by that greedy bitch Avarice. She's completely taken over what was to be a family business. The rest of us have been placed on an allowance! Everything has gone her way, our whole lives!"

"Most unfair."

"It is, yes. Anyway, I think we should get down to business. According to Aunt Demeter's monograph on the subject, optimum fertility lasts only for three days! And since the wedding, I've *wasted* seven good eggs. I want *in* the pudding club and I want in now!"

"In the pudding club?"

"You know, knocked up."

By the time she delivered that line, she'd situated herself on the pillow pyramid—her hips at the apex, well above her torso, and her legs accommodatingly splayed.

"Well, there it is," she said rather needlessly.

I set my tongue to work with the usual gusto, and she responded appreciatively. But the moment she felt herself sufficiently lubricated, she insisted I enter her. And so, enter her I did.

Whether the thought of procreation was acting as a sort of metaphysical aphrodisiac—or the three plates of oysters a gastronomic one—I couldn't be sure. But never had I managed to perform this stage for the extended duration I did that evening. Ironically, rather than being pleased, she seemed annoyed.

"Come on—quickly! The sooner we finish this round, the sooner we can have another!"

I can't say I found her attitude in any way stimulating. But soon after, I completed my husbandly duty—then promptly collapsed.

"No! No!" she shouted. "Lift up my feet! We need to help them find their way."

I did as she asked, and remained in that awkward position for some ten minutes, at which point I convinced her that being Navy men, my homunculi would have swum the distance in half that time.

"Rest for an hour," she told me. "Then you can send the next wave of Marines ashore...."

Her timing sounded a bit optimistic. I called down to the galley and asked them to send up a dozen oysters.

"And three chocolate éclairs!"

"And three chocolate éclairs," I repeated into the phone.

It was only after four additional plates of oysters (and twelve éclairs) that I was finally able to sneak away. Or, to be precise, eight and a half éclairs. Envy had fallen asleep with her legs raised high against a wall and the last éclair still dangling from her mouth. I can't say the position looked comfortable, but her expression was one of contentment.

Though it was well past three in the morning, Achilles greeted me in my sitting room.

"You look all in, sir."

"Never marry a Mortal Sin, Achilles."

"Sound advice, I'm sure. But in the heat of passion, one rarely hews to sound advice. Might I be so bold as to ask if that is what happened in your case?"

"No—cold, hard calculation. I was bargaining for the return of a consignment of liquor the mad Captain Bonnet had stolen from me."

"It must have been *very fine* liquor."

"It was. Of course, Bonnet cheated me. I didn't get back the fine liquor. And instead of three Virtues, two Muses, and two Sins, I wound up with two Muses and *five* Sins. In place of Faith, Hope, and Fortitude, I'd been saddled with Pride, Envy, and Sloth."

"Lady Sloth, at least, is generally agreeable."

"True. But Pride by herself easily makes up for her. Say, would you mind drawing me a bath?"

"Not in the least—were that lady herself not doing so already."

II

"Pride's drawing my bath?"

"Yes, most ironic, isn't it? She said she wanted you as fresh as possible, as she anticipated a busy night ahead."

"Oh. Tell me, is there another room I could sneak off to?"

I'd just finished speaking when the door to the bath opened. The embodiment of vanity stood before us in a robe even skimpier than the one she'd donned for dinner.

"You may go," she told Achilles.

"Very good, madam. Good night, sir. And you, Lady Pride."

He gave her a little bow and made his exit.

I'd only spent one night with Pride since our marriage, and that was a very active night indeed. I doubt I'd survive another such night given the condition I was in at that moment. The fact her sister Wrath wouldn't be joining us this time may have bumped the odds some, but not enough to lift my feeling of impending doom.

"You're looking well," I told her.

"Yes, I know." She eyed me suggestively, then playfully licked her upper lip. "And you... You're looking... good enough."

I know that doesn't sound like much of a compliment. But when the speaker is a Deadly Sin, one must take compliments as they come.

"Now, let's see if we can't clean that slattern off of you."

Once I'd stripped and entered the bath, she knelt behind me and ran a sponge over my arms and shoulders. Quite unexpectedly, she kissed the back of my neck, then moved alongside the tub and sponged my legs and lower torso. She was quite thorough, but uncharacteristically gentle—as if she realized what a delicate state I was in. There was no erotic handling of my still-sensitive nether regions, but three times she stopped to plant soft kisses on my lips. I wouldn't call the kisses entirely chaste, but neither were they flagrantly lewd— moderately lascivious, perhaps.

After the sponging, there was some gentle kneading of my shoulders, and several more kisses on the back of my neck. Then came the drying off. As she toweled me, I felt her lips pressing tenderly against my arms and legs. But once again, she stopped well short of my drooping mooring mast.

She was a fascinating girl, all right. At our first bout, she'd felt a need to prove she could be as invigorating as Wrath. On this occasion, she'd set herself another goal: bringing me back to working order. And she did it with a care and a patience she'd never before exhibited.

She led me by the hand into the bedroom and there dropped her gown. Then she pushed me onto the bed and continued with the ministrations—the kisses coming ever more dogged, and ever nearer my convalescing soldier.

I thought I knew what was coming next. But she'd decided to give her lips a rest, and began drawing her breasts about my belly and chest. Once in reach, I brought my mouth to the nearest. She placed a hand behind my head and clasped me to her.

It was probably two full hours before we got to the serious business, first her on mine, then me on hers. And only then the act which was her objective all along. Unlike her sister, she made no demand for encores—which would have been quite out of the question regardless. Instead, she fell asleep in my arms, looking every bit as content as Envy had earlier—though without the éclair protruding from her mouth.

When I woke to Achilles' knock, I was alone.

"Good morning, sir. I've brought you coffee. And taken the liberty of ordering breakfast—a mushroom omelet, ham, fried potatoes, and a fruit cup. I hope that meets with your approval."

"Yes, I'm starving. What time is it?"

"About two in the afternoon. We'll be mooring shortly in Tortuga. Will you be going into town?"

"No, I think I'll stay aboard. Personally, I can take or leave pirate havens."

"Indeed. Why go *out* for wicked women and cutthroats, when you have all you need at home?"

"Yes. Speaking of whom, has anyone been looking for me?"

"Lady Envy insisted that I report to her the moment you awake. Oh, and the mother-to-be you came on board with stopped by. She asked me to tell you she'd be in the library."

"Thank you. By the way, hers isn't one of mine."

"So the lady herself told me."

"Did she?"

"Seems to feel a need to explain that to everyone she meets. And that she's the wife of Captain Tigue. What she hasn't explained, if you'll pardon my curiosity, is why she's here and not with him."

"All she told me was that it's complicated."

"Indeed. Such situations usually are."

"What situations?"

"Well, for instance, those in which a woman, heavy with child, leaves her husband in the company of another man."

"Don't jump to any conclusions. She's a friend. And I ran into her *after* she'd left her husband."

"Very good, sir."

I suppose I should have boxed his ears for making insolent suggestions. But never having had a servant before, I wasn't sure when protocol demanded a demonstration of corporal punishment. I'll bet proper English gentlemen learn the art as soon as they can wield a stick.

Achilles had appraised my condition correctly, of course. Having been put through my paces the night before, I made short work of the breakfast he'd ordered. I declined, however, his offer of a combination codpiece–ice pack.

"Are you sure? Old Bill Grigson swore by them."

"The buggy-whip magnate? Did he have a harem?"

"Bill wasn't my employer. He was a sort of handy-man about the estate. A gray-haired gent. He had no wives at all—but a *very* full social calendar."

Before leaving, I instructed Achilles to keep the door locked, then had him check the hall. The coast clear, I quickly made my way to the library. It was in about the same place as previously, but had been transformed into the sort of library you'd find in a Fifth Avenue mansion. Dark oak shelving stretched floor to ceiling in a large, nine-sided room. Halfway up, a sort of mezzanine ran the entire circumference, with arches of ornately carved woodwork demarcating the turns at the corners. The vaulted ceiling bore a fresco showing the nine Muses musing in a forest populated by satyrs, centaurs, nymphs, and others of my in-laws. And they all seemed to be having a very good time.

Eugenia was seated at a massive table, so thoroughly lost in her reading she hadn't noticed me enter.

"Found something interesting?"

"Oh!" she piped.

"Sorry, didn't mean to startle you."

"That's all right. I was rather engrossed. Clio found me that trilogy of your cousin's.... You know, it's all very odd."

"If you someday meet the author, you won't need to

ask why. Is it her style of writing you find off-putting?"

"It certainly is unique. But then there's the story itself."

"Did she get any of it right?"

"Well, you have to understand that at the time, I was just a baby. From what I *can* tell, she has the general outline correct. It's just that many of her characterizations are nearer to caricatures. She makes my mother out to be a regular she-dragon."

"And she's not like that?"

"I'll grant she's a very determined woman...."

"But not so Machiavellian as Cousin Emmie makes her out?"

"Oh, Machiavelli wasn't quite as ruthless as people seem to think."

"You've read him?"

"Well, Mother suggested I should.... But really, that doesn't mean she went around *poisoning* people."

"Does Emmie have her poisoning people?"

"Not so far. But I'm only partway through the second book."

"Well, I won't spoil it for you by revealing the ending—but I *can* tell you it doesn't get any less odd."

"I've been taking some notes. I was wondering if you might be able to forward them to your cousin."

"It's not as easy as you might think. But I can try."

"And I wonder.... Oh, I suppose that would be too fantastic...."

"What?"

"Well, if she got the first batch of documents in 1903, I'd like this to arrive as near as possible to that."

"Go back in time? That might be a harder nut to crack."

"Yes—but *if* possible?"

"Yes, if possible. But remember, you'll still need to send that first batch to her from 1959. If Emmie doesn't get that, the whole project will never get off the ground—not that anyone would notice."

"But I don't even have it all yet."

"Well, you've got thirty-four years to gather it. Then it's just a matter of sending it back to that address in Brooklyn I gave you."

"To arrive in February 1903. You know, I find if I think about it too much, it gives me a headache."

"And you haven't even met Cousin Emmie yet."

"No. And probably never will."

"By the way, where's Clio?"

"She wanted to go into town for supplies. She offered to take me along, but said I might find it a little rough. Have you been to Tortuga before?"

"Yes, and unless you have a hankering for foul odors and bodily injury, you were right to forgo the experience."

"Is it that bad?"

"On my last visit, my hostess arranged to have me auctioned."

"Not very hospitable."

"No. What was it Clio needed so badly she'd venture into that snake pit?"

"Ink for her stamps. But she did take a servant with her. One of those men they call myrmidons. Do you think they're really myrmidons?"

"I'm not sure how you authenticate semi-mythical warriors—but it wouldn't surprise me if they are."

"How fascinating. And Clio, is she..."

"A real Muse? Seems to know her stuff."

"Yes. It's just that I don't remember ever hearing of the Muses getting pregnant. But there are so many versions of the myths.... Are you looking forward to having children?"

"Speaking broadly, I'm game. But when the mother-to-be is the Mortal Sin of Wrath, it would be difficult to pretend the prospect didn't instill a certain anxiety. How about you?"

"Well, likewise—speaking broadly, yes. But I would have liked it not to have occurred so unexpectedly.... Oh! Not that I'm blaming anyone!"

She was blushing. I changed the subject by asking her about her childhood.

"In most ways, idyllic. I'm the only child of a doting father and a mother who treated me more as a companion than a daughter."

"Sounds fun."

"It was, mostly. But there are times when one wants to be treated as a child. How was yours?"

"I was orphaned by nine—but it wasn't as bad as it sounds. After that, my siblings and I lived with a permissive aunt."

"Jack was an orphan from the time he was just a tot."

"But his father—"

"Oh, don't ever mention his father!"

"Sorry."

"That should never have made it into print. *The Circensiad* really wasn't meant for publication."

I almost pointed out that none of Emmie's books seemed meant for publication, but I feared she might take the criticism personally. We had afternoon tea with Clio in the librarian's private quarters, then they both begged off my company to attend to their work.

I still wasn't feeling up to another round with Envy or Pride, so I went to a part of the ship they weren't likely to visit: the engine room. This too had been upgraded, the new steam pistons much quieter than the old ones. Horatio had told me they were also more powerful. But when I asked how the steam was produced, he insisted no one knew. Given Cousin Emmie's fanciful idea of physics, I saw no point in conjecturing.

At the far end of the room—past all the pistons, gears, and rods—I came upon a little alcove. It was piled knee-deep in cushions. A small shelf held a carafe of wine and a single glass. It seemed as if someone had thought-fully provided a haven for me. I took a sip of the wine. It was a dry burgundy, quite tasty. I finished the glass and refilled it.

III

I woke with a start—but a pleasant sort of start. Someone was doing unto me as I've done to so many. And she was doing it quite ably.

I glanced down and saw a bobbing head beneath a sea of long black hair. It could only have been Sloth—but an unusually peppy Sloth. I let her proceed without interruption until I was nearly at the brink, then I reached down and pulled her up. She had on the wicked-est smile I'd ever seen. No, wicked isn't quite right. Wantonly wayward is nearer the mark. Her almond eyes looked as sleepy as always, but given that smile, and the vigorous way she rubbed my chest with hers, I'd say she was quite definitely in a wakeful mood.

I tried maneuvering down so I could repay her

kindness, but she grabbed my wrists to prevent my doing so.

"Our time may be brief," she whispered breathlessly. She always spoke somewhat breathlessly, as even the slightest exertion seemed to fatigue her. But this time there was a dimension of sensuality to it.

She brought my unbending resolve past the gates of heaven and heaved a sigh—then shook herself awake. Slowly, her hips began to undulate, and she began reciting verses in what may have been Japanese. Each one was exactly seventeen syllables, and at its conclusion, she'd let out a lustful laugh. All very erotic, which partly accounts for my going off so soon. I believe she finished then as well—assuming her climactic yawn wasn't wholly from exhaustion.

Somehow, she'd managed to fall asleep while still astride me. I carefully slipped out and turned her on her back. It was as easy as moving a slumbering cat. After placing a stack of pillows under her legs for efficacy, and another under her head for comfort, I gave her a kiss good-bye. Like her two sisters, she looked the picture of contentment—though to be honest, she rarely looked otherwise when dozing.

I was still musing upon her when the pistons suddenly burst into action. Apparently, they were only quieter when the ship was idling in port. Now that we were under way, the clatter was deafening and at least as loud as before the refitting. Sloth, however, showed no sign of stirring.

She and I had never before completed the act proper, and I felt relieved to finally be able to cross that item off the marital program. Allowing seven months to pass without getting around to the consummation had made me feel a slacker. Even if it wasn't by choice.

Though I can't claim I'd had much of a workout, I left the bridal bower feeling once again ravenous. Still hoping to avoid the others of the estrual wives, I took the stairs up to my cabin's deck—not realizing it was twenty-three flights until I arrived. Instead of a number, each floor was given a name. My deck was Verrius Flaccus, named for a Roman who'd created a combination Latin dictionary and grammar. According to the informational plaque, this magnum opus ran to twenty volumes, though only brief snippets survived. Clio, I assumed, had handed out the names.

I arrived at my floor dead beat. After a brief rest, I scanned up and down the hallway. There seemed no one about, so I made a beeline to my cabin, key in hand. It was unlocked.

Had Achilles simply forgotten my instructions, or was something far more sinister afoot? I didn't have much time to consider the point, as a hand had instantaneously shot out the door and grabbed onto to my wrist. It was a distinctly feminine hand, and yet a hand with the strength of a blacksmith's. Ergo, the hand of a Mortal Sin.

"There you are, my dear."

It was Pride, and she was dressed even more invitingly than she had been the night before, in a sheer silk negligee that covered not one percent of her shapely body.

She was not, however, alone in the room. In one corner, Envy lay on her stomach—hog-tied, gagged, and blindfolded. And in another, Achilles situated similarly. He looked to be either passed out or dead. The captive Sin, on the other hand, rolled about furiously trying to free herself.

"I thought I'd make sure I got you first this time. Shall we go into the bedchamber, where we can be alone?"

I considered using my recent liaison with Sloth as an excuse. But I decided against it for two reasons. First, Mortal Sins nearly always object when you contradict their wishes. And nine times out of ten, they make clear their objection via some variety of sharp object. Second, this particular Sin really knew how to present her form to advantage. By her rolling gait alone, she soon cast a spell over me. And like an obedient myrmidon, I followed her into the bedroom.

She fell onto the bed—lying on her back, knees up and thighs parted.

"This time, I'd like the full treatment."

Well... she got it.

Previous to our recent entente, we'd only spent that one night together—that very energetic affair that included not only her sister Wrath, but also the provoking perfume, *Deux nuits d'excès*. And from which I'd only barely emerged alive. Given the change in circumstances, I wasn't altogether sure what to expect from her during my ministrations.

"Oh, yes! Isn't it divine! Oh... Oh... Yes! Have you ever seen such a specimen?"

At first, I wasn't sure what *it* she was referring to. But once she began using proper Latin terms, I realized the *its* (for by then there had been several) were the very anatomical features my tongue was currently exploring. I'd met plenty of women well acquainted with their gadgetry—some on very intimate terms. But never one so enormously pleased with her parts. Not even the hotel manager's wife back in New York, whose plentiful punt was manned by a veritable Paul Bunyan of a boatman.

After paying homage to the essential bits, I did likewise to nipples, bum, toes, elbows—the whole gamut. Oddly, they all seemed to excite her equally. It was while I sucked on a toe that she gave out a shriek that could easily have woken the dead.

"Oh, glorious digit! Is there a supplicant, a sandal, or even a bejeweled slipper worthy of your company?"

Like all her questions that evening, this appeared to be a purely rhetorical one. Neither the toe nor I made answer.

Once my skittering tongue had attended to the last bit of her surface area, she told me it was time to render my final verdict. Not surprisingly, my erupting tribute only confirmed her own assessment.

"Oh, heavenly womb! Take what is rightfully yours!"

And with that, she collapsed.

Frankly, I didn't blame her. I may have done the majority of the physical labor, but she put twice the energy into her exaltations of self.

I dressed, then went out and untied Achilles. It turned out he was merely playing dead.

"I thought it the only safe course."

"Probably wise. How is it you let Pride subdue you?"

"I didn't. Envy ambushed me in the hall and tied me up. Then Pride ambushed her."

"You must be twice her size. I thought you myrmidons were supposed to be formidable warriors?"

"Oh, we are—as a class."

"Just not you personally."

"I do have other qualities." He looked wounded.

"Yes, I'm sure you do."

Through all of this, Envy was bucking and twisting about on the floor.

"Shouldn't we untie her?" Achilles asked.

"Why don't I leave that to you?"

I believe he started on a counter-proposal, but by then I'd left the room. I took the elevator down to the galley deck. Dinner had already been served and cleared, but the leftovers were copious. I devoured half a roast turkey and an equal portion of chestnut stuffing. Reynard had made ice cream for dessert, but there was little of that to be had. Instead I had to make do with some day-old raspberry tarts.

"I heard every damn word!"

It was Envy. How she tracked me down so quickly, I don't know. Mere logical conjecture, perhaps.

"Oh, hello. I was intending on stopping by your place later on. As to what went on upstairs, well, I wasn't given much choice."

"Liar! I heard it all."

"You heard Pride."

"Yes, but it was you making a goddess of her! What does she have that I haven't got?"

The quick answer would have been a shapely body and pride in her appearance. But by then, Envy was wielding a cleaver. So a little dissembling seemed in order.

"Nothing! Nothing at all. And how I'd like to prove it to you!"

"Well, there's no time like the present."

She cleared the large table I'd been eating at with impressive alacrity. Salvers, plates, glassware—all went flying about the room. Then she doffed the robe and positioned herself as the special of the day. I actually felt a little sorry for her. Her sisters each held supremacy in some sphere, but it was her lot to always be coveting.

While I've never been much for charity work, having been restored by my meal, I felt in a giving mood. And honestly, she did have a sort of homey charm about her.

I began at the bottom—her bottom. As it happened, she'd plopped it down on the last of the raspberry tarts. I rolled her over, and while I licked up the last of the dessert, my fingers played a tune about her forward hatch. It seemed to please her. She began mewing, though sometimes it was more of a whimper, like a child wanting comfort and affection. Why I found that erotic is probably a question best left unanswered. But I did. And I made that quite clear to her.

As far as the geographical exploration went, it was more or less a replay of my bout with sister Pride. And this time she seemed in no hurry during the final round, which was well because I was once more unusually long at it. Perhaps there were oysters in that dressing along with the chestnuts.

When I left her, she was again smiling contentedly— this time with her legs propped up against a stack of crates I'd assembled.

Chapter 8.

Fandango in Trinidad

I arrived at my apartment that evening a spent man. In the previous twenty-odd hours, I'd been put to the test no fewer than nine times, in five separate bouts, involving three different wives. I won't pretend I got nothing for my trouble—amongst the trials were numerous instances of purest ecstasy. But a man can have enough even of purest ecstasy, and at that moment, I was that man.

The door was locked. Before inserting my key, I placed an ear to it and listened. I could hear Achilles humming to himself. I rapped lightly and he unlocked and then opened the door.

"No need to fear, sir. We are, for the nonce, alone."

"That's swell—for the nonce. How about drawing me a bath while I dispense the brandy?"

"Immediately, sir."

I relocked the door, then poured us each a generous snifter-full. I drained and refilled mine twice before he returned.

"Your bath will be ready presently. It has been a taxing reunion for you, sir, hasn't it?"

"Taxing is hardly the word. But a man must do what a man must do."

"You speak like a true soldier, sir. You must have been an admirable officer."

"Well, I always had a talent for speaking like one. It was the other facets of the job where I sometimes fell a little short."

"But a man who can inspire with words is worth an army of swordsmen."

"Yes, I suppose so. Though to be perfectly honest, most of my speechifying went toward self-promotion and deflecting blame rather than inspiring."

"Your candor does you credit, sir. It takes a big man to acknowledge his shortcomings."

"You're pretty good at this toadying, aren't you?"

"One endeavors to please." There was a slight peevishness to his tone.

"Yes, of course. You're an admirable myrmidon, Achilles."

"Thank you, sir."

He went briefly into the bathroom, then returned to inform me that my bath was ready.

"Wonderful. Do you think that lock will hold?"

"I believe, sir, that neither lady left here in a condition conducive to amorous enterprises. I had to carry Lady Pride to her quarters, and Lady Envy had quite exhausted herself in struggling with her restraints."

"That's what you think. She met me down in the galley, quite in the mood for amorous enterprises."

"How did you evade her?"

"Evade her? One doesn't evade a Mortal Sin, Achilles. One merely hopes to survive the encounter."

"And you've five of them.... Tell me, sir, is that why you abandoned them?"

"There were two sides to that abandonment. But if the trials had been limited to the marriage bed, I might never have left. It was all the petty little things—all the bickering, and ridicule.... And being made to walk the plank."

"Being made to walk the plank?"

"Yes—stark naked. And six thousand feet over the

rocky coast of Maine, while Wrath lashed me with a horsewhip."

"That *is* taking fun a bit far.... But your bath, sir. It will be getting cold."

I fell asleep soaking. Sometime later, Achilles woke me and helped me to bed.

I slept fitfully after that. Every time I heard a noise, I felt a need to investigate. But there were no visitors that night. Only the sounds of an airship under way.

When Achilles brought me my tray the next morning, I was already awake.

"Good news, sir. We'll be arriving in Martinique in an hour, and Ladies Pride and Envy threw up their breakfast."

"Is that good news? I mean, their throwing up."

"They took it as confirmation they'd conceived."

"It shows itself that fast, does it? Well, good. How about Sloth?"

"Lady Sloth, from my understanding, dines only once a day. Just after sunset."

"Ah. Crepuscular, like a cat. Let's hope she has an after-dinner hairball today."

Once *Lucy* had moored, I escorted Eugenia to the French Line's ticket office where she secured a berth on the airship leaving the next day. Back outside, she handed me the packet she'd prepared for Emmie.

"I thought you could address it. I think delivery in 1908 would be ideal, but any time before 1910 and after 1905 would be acceptable."

"All right, I'll see what I can manage. Shall I take you to a hotel?" I asked.

"God, no! ...I mean... no, thank you. That won't be necessary. I can take a cab."

"Well, good-bye, and good luck." I held out my hand, and she took it in hers.

"You must promise not to tell Jack where I've gone."

"OK, if that's what you want."

"Or Marpesia—should you run into her."

"That's not very likely. But you can count on me."

"Oh. There's something else I wanted to ask your opinion on. I've been trying to think of a name."

"A name?"

"For the baby."

"Oh."

"Not that it should matter to you, of course."

"No, of course. Well, how about Jack?"

"Jack? No, I wouldn't want him to... You know."

"I suppose it does sound a little piratical. Then how about Bill? Nice sort of insurance broker name."

"Yes, that's good. I like William. And if it's a girl?"

"Ah... How about Willie? Keep things simple."

"*Willie?*"

"I knew a girl named Willie when I was stationed in Norfolk."

"What sort of girl was she?"

"Don't really know. We never hit it off. She spent a lot of time at church."

"Oh. That's OK then."

While she jotted something in her little notebook, I procured her a cab. Then she once more took my hand in hers.

"Well, good-bye," she said. "And thank you.... I mean, for helping me out...."

"Glad to be of service.... I mean, to have helped.... Well..."

There are certain situations when nearly anything

can seem an innuendo, and this was one of them. Luckily, Eugenia cut it short by giving me a quick peck on the
cheek and boarding the cab.

Just to set the record straight, I'd given her the
name Willie as something of a lark. Only years later did I
find out she actually used it. If I ever meet that child, I
expect she's going to want some explanations....

My wives spent the day shopping and arrived back
at the ship that evening with several hampers full of
French delicacies, a dozen bolts of silk, two midwives,
and a nearsighted obstetrician named Armida. The
doctor hailed from the Levant originally, a short, fat,
olive-skinned woman who claimed powers beyond what's
taught in medical school. I sat beside her at dinner and
discovered she had a truly wicked sense of humor.
Whether that would stand her in good stead with the
wives remained to be seen.

The midwives were a pair of comely twins named
Georgette and Philippa, not much older than eighteen.
They were native Martiniquais, with large eyes, bright
smiles, and flawless skin. I offered to show them around
the ship after dinner and they jumped at the opportunity—as did Armida, the chaperone they insisted on bringing. It turned out these two were even more devoted to
their Savior than that Willie back in Norfolk. I found
them pleasant enough, but I've always gotten along
better with Catholic girls who arrive pre-fallen. Coaxing
them over the precipice comes too close to work.

Ironically, it looked as if I'd be spending a quiet
night alone. But when I reached my apartment, I found
Sloth leaning against the door sound asleep. Apparently,
she hadn't had the same sort of confirmation Pride and
Envy had. I woke her with a kiss and helped her inside. I

called for Achilles, but soon happened upon a note reminding me this was his evening off. Poor timing, I thought. We were already under way for Port of Spain and he'd have few options for entertainment.

As we crossed the threshold into the bedroom, Sloth kissed me lovingly. Sleepily too, but warm and wet enough to allow the amorous intent primacy. What sex we had that night came slow and intermittent, with frequent naps breaking the action. Normally, I would have found the regime more than a little frustrating. But that night, it suited me as much as it did her. Though my desire appeared to have recovered nicely, my body was still in a recuperative state.

The sun had risen when I at last cast my seed. She received it eagerly, then drowsily, and by the end, only barely awake.

Afterward, sleeping blissfully, she looked the very picture of contentment. Even the periodic snorts failed to mar the effect. In an effort to facilitate the hoped-for conception, I turned her one hundred and eighty degrees about and braced her legs up against the wall. She snored without interruption throughout the maneuver.

Later that morning, Avarice requested I join her for breakfast in her quarters. The request arriving in the form of two burly myrmidons.

"I've laid out a campaign of action," she informed me.

"A campaign of action?"

"To bring Myra back in line. I told you about that when you boarded. Don't you ever listen?"

"Sorry, I've been rather busy of late...."

"Yes, banging your wives and trying to get under the skirts of those midwives."

"Believe me, the banging of wives was by command. As for those girls, I was just being hospitable."

"Well, leave them alone—or I'll have Armida put a curse on your little friend." She pointed vaguely toward my midsection.

"Little?"

"*Oh, please.* Set your libido aside for a moment and listen. My plan is to approach Myra in much the same way we did last time."

"Isn't that likely to result in much the same outcome: me being beaten and thrown into a fetid puddle of human waste?"

"The difference is, this time I will go first and present my terms. She, of course, will call out her goons. Only then will you arrive—*with* a dozen myrmidons in tow. Her handful of thugs will be no match for our professionals. *She'll have to fall in line!*"

"Is her place so lucrative it's worth all this trouble?"

"What trouble? What's the point of hiring automatons if you don't make use of them? Besides, if we don't persuade her to come back into the fold, we might face rebellions elsewhere. That overripe peach in Port Royal is just waiting for an opportunity to cut loose. We must make an example of this damned Myra."

I left her carrying detailed instructions and feeling something like a member of the Tsar's secret police. Making examples out of people wasn't something I could raise much enthusiasm for. Perhaps because, more often than not, I'd been on the receiving end.

I returned to my apartment just as Achilles arrived. He looked all in. Actually, worse than all in.

"Where have you been?"

"I'd prefer not to have to divulge that."

"Oh. All right..."

"Well, if you must know, sir, I was ambushed!"

"*Ambushed?* Not getting along with the other fellows?"

"Oh, not by myrmidons. By those two midwives!"

"Georgette and Philippa? Didn't seem the ambushing type to me."

"Nor me, sir. I passed them in the hall and they asked if I could bring a bottle of wine to their room. It seemed not an unreasonable request, so I complied. On entering, they fell upon me!"

"Really? They seemed the knees-locked-shut sort of girls to me."

"A mere act, I'm afraid. They were like a pair of tigresses."

"Well, petite tigresses like them should have been easy to fend off."

"True, sir. But we myrmidons are conditioned from birth to please. By adulthood, it becomes instinct."

"So you followed your instinct?"

"In truth, my instinct followed theirs. You see, they knew quite a bit about pleasing as well."

"Then it must not have been all bad."

"Oh, not at all, sir. But when I left them, three or four hours ago, I needed to pass by the lady doctor's door...."

"Armida? Did she put a charm on you?"

"No, something more akin to a headlock." He paused to rub his neck. "With her, the pleasing was rather one-sided."

It was a blow to the ego, having my servant succeed where I'd failed. But there's no disputing that myrmidons exude that he-man aspect that many women find alluring. Achilles may have been the least he-mannish of the lot, but even he ranked well above your average college fullback. I suggested he take a long bath and went off to find Horatio.

I found him reading a newspaper in the apartment he shared with Mattie—and her actually sewing on a button. Both had put on a few pounds since our last voyage together. Age—and the French pastries—seemed to be catching up with them.

Mattie poured me coffee and offered a plate of chocolate croissants. They were fresh and irresistible.

II

Achilles' account had fixed my thoughts on a question I'd hitherto assiduously avoided. No doubt it's crossed your mind as well. Here were seven young, healthy women, apparently abandoned by their husband. And with them were a dozen subservient he-men raised from birth to please in every way possible.

Mattie was not a woman to feign innocence, so I posed my query rather bluntly.

"Ain't been none of that," Horatio told me. "Least since we been aboard."

"I don't want to appear the jealous ogre. But you must admit, it is a little surprising. I mean, five of them are Mortal Sins, who rarely show much hesitation when it comes to feeding yens. And when I came aboard, three were in heat!"

"Oh, a Sin is a curious creature," Mattie said. "'Course I don't need to tell *you* that...."

"No, they're curious, all right. But they don't seem too worried about eternal damnation and things of that sort."

"Well, could be those myrmidons just don't appeal to them," he conjectured. "You know, I had one helpin' me in the engine room the other day and there was an accident. Put his hand where he shouldn't have—little finger got sliced clean off. He didn't even notice 'til I pointed it out to him."

"Don't feel no pain, those myrmidons," Mattie confirmed. "Other day, I saw one pull a potato out of a pot of boiling water like it was nothing at all."

"So you think the fact they don't feel pain has something to do with the Sins not partaking of them?"

"Could be. Seein' you in pain always puts a smile on their faces."

"I suppose that's as good an explanation as any."

"'Course, we could be wrong," he went on. "But once the babies start poppin' out, we can tell who's been givin' the double-shuffle."

"Oh, if there's been any of that, we'll need to abandon ship," Mattie told him. "Can you imagine—half Sin, half myrmidon?"

It certainly was a scary thought.

That evening, when Sloth threw up her dinner, there was much joy about the ship. I had Achilles break open a case of champagne, but the womenfolk—all except Mattie, Armida, and the two midwives—begged off. My wives took their maternal responsibilities quite seriously.

I hoped that boded well for the characters of their progeny. After all, could a child bathed in love and devotion evolve into a second coming of Wrath? (I guess it all depended on whether the mythical mandates were hereditary, a point of supposition not yet settled.)

We arrived in Port of Spain late that evening. Avarice promptly went off to The Ugly Toucan, Myra's establishment, accompanied by just one of the myrmidons. Ten minutes later, I set off with the balance. Her plan sounded a little too confrontational for my taste. But there is something to be said for directing operations from behind a wall of mindless automatons incapable of feeling pain.

Our route took us along the waterfront. About half-way to the rendezvous, we came upon a commotion. A gaggle of rough-looking characters was giving three ladies a difficult time. Voices were raised, and several cutlasses as well.

"Someone ought to teach those hooligans a lesson," I said to Achilles.

I was speaking rhetorically, as I usually do in such situations, and in a low voice—just in case said hooligans might overhear me and take offense. But, apparently, not so low that the other myrmidons didn't pick up on my words.

You don't come across many myrmidons capable of appreciating the subtle inflections of intonation which distinguish a rhetorical comment. I had hardly finished my sentence before my own band of hooligans fell upon the seafaring hooligans—Achilles excepted. Not only could he appreciate the subtle inflections of intonation, he was, as I would learn presently, every bit the coward I was.

The fray encompassed an impressive variety of bloodletting skills. It reminded me of the one I'd watched from the auction block back on Tortuga, when the Amazons and La Baza's men went at it in Dead Man's Cove. Though to be honest—and I say this as a great admirer of women—one myrmidon can wreak three times the carnage of the fiercest Amazon. And so they demonstrated that evening in Port of Spain.

In numbers, the two sides began evenly matched. But soon a large wave of ruffians emerged from their ship to join the fight. Most died quickly, though a few held on for a minute or two. Our side also took some hits, of course. But unless you literally disarm a myrmidon, he's very difficult to discourage. And removing the arms—or any limb—from such a giant is no mean feat.

"Come on, you nancies! Fight like men!"

That was the ruffian captain voicing encouragement to his men. I doubt he recognized me, as I'd pretty effectively shielded myself from the action behind a screen of barrels. But I recognized him, all right. It was La Baza, the Cyclops and erstwhile captor of Clematis, my onetime concubine and the doppelganger of my former supposed wife, who was now sojourning safely in non-fictional Washington, D.C.

He was about as large as a myrmidon, and a good deal more bloodthirsty. But while he was leading his life of rapaciousness, the myrmidons had been working out. One of them picked the brute up and flung him skyward. He landed on the mast of his own ship, skewered. Within seconds, the few remaining of his ruffians fled to parts unknown.

We'd won the field, though not without cost. Most of my band suffered only minor injuries—a missing foot, maybe an arm. However, their loss of blood had by then rendered them decidedly lethargic. I'd little choice but to have the walking wounded carry their comrades back to *Lucy* for repair.

The three ladies my efforts had saved from ignominious handling had likewise watched the battle from cover. They came toward me now, and I prepared myself to receive their thanks with all the humility I could muster.

"You bloody son of a bitch! Why, I oughtta ram this parasol right up your bunghole!"

Seeing them now close up, I realized I'd rescued not a trio of gentlewomen, but three draggle-tailed members of that guild known colloquially as the daughters of joy.

"Yeah! Whattaya mean, messin' with a girl's livelihood?"

The third one didn't speak to me in such aggrieved tones. She did, however, draw a dagger, which she subsequently held to my throat. "It's all right, girls. Sweetie here's goin' to make up ar lost wages. Aren't ya, Sweetie?"

I hesitated for a moment, expecting that at any second Achilles would approach from behind and disarm the wench. But once I felt blood trickling down my chest, I thought it best to be gallant and make the ladies whole. Fifteen pounds sterling it cost me—and without even benefit of their services.

A crowd had by then gathered, as La Baza's impaled body could be seen from a fair distance away. There was some jocularity vented, but far more disgust. When the tut-tutting got serious, and I could see people staring in my direction, I took the cue to make my exit and headed in the direction of The Ugly Toucan. Two blocks up the street, Achilles joined me.

"Where were you?"

"Evaluating lines of retreat."

"Evaluating, or utilizing?"

"Oh, definitely evaluating. Very thoroughly evaluating."

We entered Myra's establishment together, but by the time I was knocking on the door to her office, Achilles had once more vanished.

The proprietress greeted me warily. She still thought

I was Smedley at this point, and there seemed to be the hint of some lingering affection about her eyes—though she may have just had a bad night's sleep.

Avarice was on the other side of the room with her unconscious myrmidon lying on the floor beside her. Myra's hired thugs surrounded them.

"*Where have you been?*" my greedy one growled. "And *where* are my men?"

"There's good news and bad news on that front...."

Before I could continue, an auxiliary thug rushed in and whispered something in Myra's ear. Her expression turned to one of alarm, whereupon her eyes met mine.

"*You did what?*"

My blood—as it is wont to do in such situations—turned cold.

III

The soul-piercing glare Myra was casting my way concerned me. Her eyes now betrayed neither affection nor sleep deprivation. They seemed to be protruding an inch or so beyond their respective sockets.

"Tell me now! Is it true that fiend La Baza is dead?"

Needless to say, her choice of descriptor came as a huge relief.

"He is indeed, skewered on his very own mast."

"And... you did that?"

"I had little choice! The man had crossed me one time too many. I caught his band molesting maids dockside."

"You haven't answered *my* question!" the personification of greed interjected. "*Where are my men?*"

"Well, as I mentioned earlier, there's both good

news and bad news. The vanquishing of the tyrant is the former...."

"How many dead?"

"None—last I saw them. And most still had the full complement of limbs."

"Not too high a price to be rid of La Baza!"

I'd made a convert of Myra.

My wife, however, thought differently: "Keep your opinions to yourself, *barkeep!*"

"Get her, and *it,* out of here!" the barkeep commanded, nodding at the slumbering myrmidon.

"You'll both of you pay for this!"

As Avarice and her bodyguard were dragged away— him still lifeless, but her kicking and screaming up a storm—Myra turned to me, teary-eyed.

"I don't know how to thank you. I've dreamed of this day!"

"No need for thanks. The pleasure was all mine." I always knew that I'd make a superb hero if given half a chance. "Had La Baza done you some personal wrong?"

"Not me. My cousin. A mere ingenue, raised on an Ohio farm. She was on her way to join me in Fort-de-France when she fell into the clutches of La Baza. Never to be seen again!"

"Ohio?"

"Yes. Why?"

"Is she about ye high, with brown eyes, chestnut hair, and a delightfully pleasing disposition?"

"Yes!"

"Answers to Clematis, or simply Clem when among friends?"

"Yes! Yes! Have you seen her? Is she... is she still..."

"Alive and well. I myself rescued her—twice. Once

off the auction block in St. Pierre, and once from La Baza's very own lair."

"Oh! Where is she now?"

"Well... she's in Washington...."

"I must write to her."

"Ah—that might not be as easy as you think."

"Why?"

"I'm afraid that explanation will require some groundwork. First of all, I'm not Smedley."

"That explains it."

"Explains what?"

"He would never do anything so noble—or so self-less."

"I know all about his selfishness."

"*You do?*" she seemed surprised, and a little put off by my answer.

"Indirectly. Through friends."

"Who precisely?"

"That matters not. For I will right that wrong as well!"

"You will?"

"Rest assured. You'll never think again of... what's-his-name." I kissed her hand. She purred.

"You may leave us," she told the underlings still in attendance.

I'd met a good number of game girls in my time. Most found me a ready source of short-term amusement, and a few even found me bearable for longer periods. But never had I encountered an attitude like Myra's. She was downright smitten. Not even Clem was smitten—only so thoroughly agreeable she sometimes came across that way. Myra fell into my arms.

I believe I mentioned before her uncanny likeness to

Aggie, and it was even more apparent now. But the similarity began and ended with the anatomy. Attitudewise, they couldn't be more different. At least in their attitude toward me.

Within seconds, I had her on the couch—skirt up and pants off. Just as I suspected, she was a novice when it came to being on the receiving end. But she learned quickly. She kneaded my scalp as I worked, then began humming. If it was one particular number, I didn't recognize it. Partly because the melody seemed to change periodically, with not even the slightest pause between. It reminded me of the overture that begins many musical comedies.

While I wouldn't call the effect arousing, the buoyant air did provide confirmation that my efforts were appreciated—and *that* I always find arousing.

She wasn't as assertive a lover as my wives, but nor was she a complacent one. When she'd had her fill of my work below deck, she kissed me lavishly about the face, sunk her tongue down my throat, and coaxed my mooring mast to where it could be of the most use to her. At this part of the game she was a natural talent, moving her hips with slight variations in direction, and then—when she sensed I'd become too fervid too soon—she'd pull away and place my head upon her breasts. They were as dainty as Aggie's, and the nipples at their centers every bit as sensitive. She giggled during this stage. Usually I find such behavior disconcerting. But hers was a suggestive, wanton sort of giggle, and it worked quite the opposite.

She kept me working most of the night. But through her artfulness, she also kept me spiritually engaged. When at last she accepted my gift, and the grunting over, we both fell into a deep, satisfied sleep.

It wasn't until after noon of the next day that we

woke. She rang a bell and ten minutes later we were brought an ample, if somewhat flavorless, breakfast. By then, I'd already decided to have a go at winning Myra's hand—or whichever parts she was willing to share. I also had a mental list running of little improvements I might make about the place—provided, of course, that she could afford them.

First on my list was to have the curtains and wallpaper replaced. I don't usually fixate on such things, but her apartment resembled a funeral parlor. One of those dark Victorian places that always smell musty. Second was to hire a French cook. There was just no denying the food aboard *Lucy* was of a superior sort. But *not* a pâtissier—I didn't want Myra becoming as chubby as my wives.

I suppose you're thinking I was getting a little ahead of myself. However, as I said before, Myra was smitten. And she wasn't a girl who did things by half measures. Over breakfast, I served up a heavily redacted version of my biography. She ate it up as readily as she did her overcooked omelet.

But when I got to the part about crossing over between worlds, she had a harder time digesting.

"Now you're starting to sound like Jules Verne, or H.G. Wells."

"I'm afraid it *is* something like that. But I don't know how I can prove it."

"It's OK. Whether that part's true, or you're just a little nutty, it doesn't matter. The important thing is you saved Clem!"

"Twice," I reminded her. "And..."

"*And* put an end to La Baza!" She then broke into hysterics.

Admittedly, I'd gotten a little carried away with the

self-aggrandizement. But I didn't mind being laughed at by Myra, regardless. For the simple reason that no matter how outrageous she found me, she remained, first and last, smitten.

By the end of the week, I'd quite comfortably settled into my new position as Myra's consort. Her minions rose to my call, and even that of *my* minion, Achilles. Better still, her banker treated me with respect. When I suggested that like my wives, we move into the field of casino gambling, she welcomed my participation and agreed enthusiastically.

It was about three weeks after my arrival that I saw a familiar face hovering over the roulette wheel. It was Kelso, the fellow Academy alum who'd brought me to Port Royal.

"You sure you should be playing?" I asked.

"Luck's bound to turn my way."

All gamblers take that attitude. And, of course, someday it does. But only the rare bird will quit while he's ahead. Kelso was not that rare bird. I extended him a generous amount of credit.

Not unexpectedly, he ended the night deep in the hole. I brought him back to the office.

"I can write you a check," he told me. "Drawn on a New York bank."

"Fictional, or real?"

"Real, I'm afraid. I keep most of my money back there. They've started taxing ill-gotten gains on this side, and since I can't account for the cash, they assume I'm rum-running! Very annoying."

"I'll tell you what. I'll run you a tab until you pass through again—*if* you'll deliver a package to the other side."

"Who to?"

"It goes to an Emily Reese, in Brooklyn."

"Ah, she of the scientifically challenged mind. Just give me the address."

"The address is on it. But the sender wishes it to arrive circa 1908."

"*1908?*"

"Yes. The reasoning is rather complicated. But anytime between, say, 1905 and 1910 would do. I thought you'd mastered the art?"

"I wouldn't say mastered. But I was thinking of making a go for the late summer of 1907—short some copper shares, maybe a few banks."

"Ah, the ole Panic of '07. Yes, that would be fine. ...Say, do you think I could invest what you owe?"

"I don't see why not."

"In that case, go on back to the tables if you'd like."

He did, of course. Ultimately, he left three thousand in the red to us.

About two weeks after that, Myra threw up her breakfast. I suggested it might be indicative of pregnancy and she seemed to warm to the idea. Marginally less so when I conjectured that the sheer quantity of egesta probably meant she was carrying twins, at the very least.

We'd settled into a comfortable existence. But there was one thing that preyed on us both: the thought of Avarice returning with her myrmidons rejuvenated. I made inquiries into getting a few of our own, but apparently that market had tightened and prices were through the roof. So we made do with a baker's dozen of Mamelukes—not quite so biddable as myrmidons, but every bit as formidable.

With safety less of a concern, I began searching for a

second location. I quickly set my sights on Curaçao. There were no competitor casinos nearby, and that mercantile colony attracted only the better-behaved class of pirate—men more interested in investing their booty than laying waste to port towns.

I had the place up and running in no time. At first, the clientele ran a little *too* mercantile-minded—if not downright tight-fisted. So I placed ads in several of the trade magazines. That was my first mistake.

The second was not recognizing Geoff l'Indigné quickly enough. (To be fair, I was distracted by several of the clients attempting to lynch the croupier at the black-jack table.) When I did set eyes on him, Geoff looked more ebullient than indignant. He cackled, naturally. Then the three men with him cackled. Then they all cackled in unison.

My third mistake actually came before the other two—I'd left all the Mamelukes in Port of Spain protecting Myra. The only member of a warrior caste I'd brought with me was Achilles. And that spineless myrmidon had disappeared before the first cackle. I tried inveigling the staff to come to my aid, but all that gained me was a sea of dubious looks and several hearty guffaws.

Geoff had his men haul me out to the street, but this being tidy Willemstad, they found no puddle of filth to toss me into. So they contented themselves with tossing me onto the pavement and dragging me by my feet to their airship. And cackling, of course.

Once aboard, I was brought to their captain's quarters. Jean Lafitte again enumerated his various grievances with me: the attack on his base at Barataria and the destruction of his auction house; the still-owed three thousand dollars for Clem; the deception involving the

Limnads; and now, the ransom I'd led him to believe Bonnet would pay for my return.

"I can't say I feel responsible for all of that, but just what sort of dollar figure are we talking about?"

"Off the top of my head—with interest and penalties—forty-seven thousand four hundred and ninety-seven."

"Well, why not keep things simple and make it an even forty-seven thousand five hundred. I'm actually doing quite well right now. If we were to stop by Port of Spain, I could make a sizable good-faith payment."

"Good-faith! Bah! I'll put an ad in the ransom columns. If someone comes up with the money, you'll be freed. In the meantime, *it's to the oars with you!*"

I didn't recognize any of the current collection of galley slaves. But I had been away for several months by then, and a galley slave's lifespan can usually be measured in weeks, if not days. Given the interval, I was somewhat out of shape and a little slow getting back up to speed. Luckily, the brute manning the lash provided me a few helpful reminders, and I was soon pulling to the beat.

I can't say for sure how long I was at it this go-round. I skipped the salmagundi the first few times it was offered and severe malnutrition has always played havoc with my sensibilities. Once I came to terms with the probable cannibalism, however, my mind returned to normal and I was able to appreciate what an utterly miserable and hopeless state I was in.

One day—or night, for a galley slave is rarely aware of the time of day—the ship was hit by something. This was about the fourth week of my second shift, and the salmagundi had been coming a little watery of late, so I was frequently falling prey to hallucinations. Nonetheless, the thud had a vaguely familiar sound to it. It was followed close on by several more thuds, and the brute with the lash opened a hatch to see what it was about.

No sooner had he done so than he was gored by the detached head of a Texas longhorn....

CHAPTER 9.

HERO FOR A DAY

"It's Jack! Jack Tigue's come to save us!" one of the living corpses on the bench opposite mine shouted. Actually, it was more of a modulated wheeze. By and large, living corpses don't do a lot of shouting.

His hypothesis echoed about the oar deck to generally favorable reviews. My personal feelings on the subject were somewhat ambivalent. While it's true Jack had a reputation for rescuing those in mortal peril, in practice, his efforts focused almost exclusively on comely young females possessed of appreciative natures. Far more worrying, he seemed to have developed a personal animus for yours truly. When last we'd met, at the Lafittes' auction house, he seemed quite content to see me executed by the highest bidder.

There was a great deal of commotion throughout the ship, and soon the battle spilled onto the oar deck. Geoff l'Indigné was fending off half a dozen of Jack's men and doing it quite ably. Blood splattered, body parts flew—and Geoff cackled. He appeared to be enjoying himself immensely. But only up to the point when Jack approached from behind and tapped him on the shoulder. Not unnaturally, the ill-timed interruption roused Geoff's abeyant indignation. He turned about and we were treated to a spirited contest of swordsmanship.

Almost immediately, Geoff scored a blow to Jack's sword arm, and had he not paused to throw back his head and cackle, I believe victory would have been his. But Geoff never could pass up an opportunity to cackle—

nor Jack one to eviscerate. The oar deck resounded with cheers, audible even above the cries of the wounded.

I'd tried keeping my face averted so as not to be recognized. But it's damned difficult remaining indifferent with a show like that going on. No sooner had Geoff's disemboweled carcass fallen to the deck than Jack's eyes met mine. He smiled—but not the sort of smile that brings cheer to the beleaguered galley slave.

"Bring him to my cabin," he told his men, whilst waving his bloody cutlass in my direction. "The rest you can set free."

I wiped away the gore he'd flung at me in preparation of returning his greeting, but he had gone. One of his men removed my shackles, then led me along passageways jammed with dismembered pirates. Eventually we came to the passage that led to Lafitte's own cabin. There the fight continued, and I could hear the Cajun cackling orders to those of his men still among the living. We crossed via a swinging gangway to Jack's ship, *The Buttered Goose*, and thence made our way to Jack's cabin. The buccaneer tied me to a chair with coarse ropes.

"Wait here," he said, then left the room cackling at his little witticism. Any boy harboring illusions about life among the pirating class ought to be made to listen to an extended concert of their cackles. If he can bear that, the privations and bloodletting will come easy.

It looked as if Jack had been interrupted mid-meal, for his desk was covered with an array of half-eaten dishes. I managed to inch the chair up nearer and sunk my face into the one platter I could now reach. It looked to be a partridge, or quail, and the aroma would certainly have made my mouth water had I not been too dehydrated to salivate. It was delicate work, avoiding the small bones without the use of my hands. But as a galley slave, one soon learns that risks must be taken at mealtime. The odds of that human dactyl having been washed prior to being tossed in the salmagundi are small indeed.

I should have avoided the tiny wings, of course, but Jack had already availed himself of the meatier pieces, and beggars can't be choosers. I'm sure I would have choked to death if someone hadn't then entered the room and whacked me on the back.

"Second time today I saved your life." It was Jack, as insufferable as ever. "Too bad if now I had to cut it short."

"I'm eternally grateful, Jack. And if there's anything I can do...."

"Just one thing. Tell me what you did with my wife."

"Look, Jack. She left you of her own accord. She wouldn't tell me why. I just assisted her as I would any friend."

"Like back in Nassau last summer?"

"No! Not like that—not that anything happened then."

"*Something* happened. But we'll get to that later. First I want you to tell me where she is now."

"I gave her my word I wouldn't, Jack."

"Not even if I untie ya and let ya finish my lunch?"

Under normal circumstances, I would have succumbed to such a temptation and told him all he wanted to know. But the delirium I'd been suffering from recently must have gained the upper hand.

"Not even then, Jack. I consider Eugenia a friend, and I'll not betray a friend."

"Gee, that's noble of you." He came around behind me and slit my bonds. "Go ahead and eat."

I did as he commanded, and quite greedily. When

I'd licked clean the last platter, he looked over at me and smiled. I was rather surprised he'd taken my refusal so well. It seemed rather unlike Jack.

"Well, now that you took a turn playin' noble, you can go back to being the miserable coward we both know ya are." During the second half of his sentence, he'd brought the tip of his cutlass against my left cheek. "*Now talk!*"

My delirium having been miraculously cured by the combination of Jack's leftovers and the point of his sword, I did as he requested.

"I took her to Martinique."

"*Why?*"

"She bought an airship ticket for Marseilles. She told me she planned on having the baby in France."

He made a noise. "Women in her family are always doin' that."

"Are they?"

"You see her aboard?"

"No, but I've no reason to think she didn't catch the flight."

"She written you from France?"

"Well, if she has, it'd be unlikely to have reached me. See, at the time, I'd briefly reconciled with my wives. A day later, they abandoned me in Port of Spain."

"So it was *you* who took up with Myra?"

"Oh. You know Myra?"

"Let's just say we're acquainted."

I can't say I was pleased to hear that. Jack's acquaintances with women rarely fell short of intimate.

"She and I have formed a sort of partnership," I told him.

"Family partnership?"

"Yes—without the formality of marriage."

"Yeah, I guess you've had your fill of that."

"I have, yes. But the responsibilities aren't shed so easily as the wives themselves."

"What the hell's that mean?"

"They're all seven in the family way."

"Jesus."

"Yes, my thoughts exactly." I couldn't discern from his expression if he was merely impressed or there was an element of jealousy included. Jack, I'd heard on good authority, was incapable of fathering children.

"Now let's get back to that night in Nassau."

"All right, Jack. But hear me out before you rush to judgment. There were certain complicating factors, which, through no fault of mine, led to unavoidable consequences."

"OK, I'll hear you out. *Then* I'll rush to judgment."

"Very droll, Jack. Well, at the time I was planning on settling down in Nassau with Gertie Littko."

"Then why weren't ya with her?"

"She had me on probation. Insisted I check in at a hotel in town. Later that same afternoon, I ran into Eugenia outside a steamship office looking forlorn. Decidedly forlorn. She was low on funds, so I bought her a meal and booked her a room at the hotel. But before her room was ready, she felt in need of a nap. So I lent her my room and went off to.... to get my hair cut, and then to Gertie's place for dinner."

"You skipped the part where you placed the ad offerin' her for sale or trade."

"Ah. Well, you see, she was anxious to hook up with that Marpesia woman. And I was hoping to see my supposed wife, who, as you know, had signed up with the

Amazons. Placing the ad seemed a clever way to get them to come to us."

"I thought you just said you were going to settle down with Gertie in Nassau?"

"Yes, but I thought I should at least take my formal leave of Sesbania."

"Jesus."

"Anyway, after my dinner with Gertie, I returned to find Eugenia packing my things."

"Why?"

"Well, since she'd slept in my bed, she thought the proper thing to do was to give me her room. Anyway, amongst my possessions she found an all-but-empty vial of perfume. Curiosity getting the best of her, she opened it and took in the last of the fumes. Such were the complicating factors. Now come the unavoidable consequences."

"I'm all ears."

"Have you ever heard of a fragrance called *Deux nuits d'excès?*"

"Doubt it. What's it mean in American?"

"Two nights of excess. It's a phenomenally powerful female aphrodisiac. Marpesia and her Amazons made use of it when they raided that steamship where Sesbania was taken. When they later boarded *Lucy's Revenge*, some of it was left behind with a defector."

"And you're sayin' this perfume causes women to... well, throw caution to the winds?"

"Under the influence of this perfume, women have no conception of caution."

"Sounds like it might be fun—or dangerous, maybe."

"Plenty of both. Sometime I'll tell you about the evening I spent with Pride and Wrath under its influence."

M.E. MEEGS

"I can't picture Eugenia dangerous whatever she sniffed."

"No, not dangerous. But determined. Believe me, Jack, she wasn't herself."

"But you *were* yourself. You could have put a stop to it."

"Not without offending her, Jack. I mean, be fair. What would you have done, supposing Eugenia were a childhood friend of mine and you a mere acquaintance?"

"You ain't no mere acquaintance—not anymore."

"I was then. Just helping a girl in need."

"Well, I'll reserve judgment for now. But it would help your case if you got ahold of some of that scent."

"The perfume? I'll see what I can do. It's precious stuff. And difficult to come by at any price."

"But Marpesia knows how to get it?"

"Apparently."

"You know, she's attacked me again—twice."

"Still trying to convert your harem?"

"No. Now it's because she thinks I have Eugenia aboard."

"So Marpesia is another of Eugenia's old friends. But not yours?"

"No. All I ever got from her was the high hat."

"She does seem rather free with the derision.... Just like my wives. Say, what about your harem? Must number in the dozens by now."

"Nope. I raided Barataria last January and put an end to the Lafittes' game once and for all. And to Pierre. Today I finished the job with Jean."

"Dead?"

"Looked that way. But it's hard takin' the pulse of a mess of guts and bones."

176

"Well, I can't say I'll miss him."

"You know, a fellow told me *you* did in La Baza. I told him he must have the wrong guy."

"As a matter of fact, I did do him in. At least, one of the family retainers did while under my direction."

"I suppose I can believe *that*. I remember now hearin' how you set out to tame the pirate menace."

"I was young and naïve then."

"What, last summer?"

"Believe me, a lot's happened since last summer."

"Maybe you should finish the job."

"You're joking, Jack."

"No, I'm not. How would you like to get credited with the Lafittes, too?"

"How do you mean?"

"You play the hero. Slayer of the Lafitte brothers, plus that bastard La Baza."

"That'd be very generous of you, Jack. What's in it for you?"

"I want you to do in one more."

"Who?"

"Me."

II

"You want me to kill you?"

"Don't be a gink. I want you to *pretend* to kill me. I've got it all planned."

"But why, Jack? You always seem to be having such a swell time."

"Just sick of doing the same thing, day after day—running rum, freeing virgins, keeping a harem happy—hell, even the gutting and maiming's gotten old."

"I had no idea, Jack.... Were they all virgins?"

"Jesus. Whattaya want, a scorecard? The point is, I've had enough. And now I've got these damn Amazons taking me on.... Every week, like clockwork!"

"Are they so much better armed than Lafitte and the rest?"

"Hell, they're women! I can't chop some girl's arm off just because she shot some hot fudge at my ship."

"I suppose it would be considered ungentlemanly."

"Say, how come you aren't worried about that supposed wife of yours? That's a rough crowd she's playing with."

"She's made her opinion of me all too clear. You remember last summer, back in Tortuga, when one of your fellows saw her board that tramp steamer?"

"Yeah—even remember its name: *The Slippery Eel*."

"Yes. Well, that wasn't Sesbania, that was her double. Sesbania spent that night with me pretending to be the double. Then the next morning, in Nassau, she went on the lam."

"Jesus. That must be when she got knocked up."

"Sesbania? When'd you hear she was pregnant?"

"A while ago. Late March, maybe. They tried another boarding party and we captured a few more of them."

"Are they still aboard?"

"No, they said they'd had enough of pirating. I fronted them the cash to open a speakeasy in Chicago. If you pass through there, look them up. Said they'd name it The Buttered Goose."

"I will. I suppose I should thank you for not attacking and possibly killing my supposed wife and putative child."

"It's on the house. Now let's get back to the plan. I

met this guy in a bar in Havana, a former Navy man like you. We got talking shop, and he told me he could get ahold of something that would make a boiler explosion seem like a champagne cork popping. Comes in a bottle, he said."

"Nitroglycerin?"

"Didn't catch what he called it."

"What about his name? Wouldn't happen to be Kelso, would it?"

"Yeah. You know him?"

"Yes. Went to the same school. I ran into him a couple months back myself—made an investment with him."

"Yeah? Me too. Anyway, I'm supposed to meet him in Havana tomorrow."

"And he's going to give you the nitroglycerin then?"

"Sell. That's the plan. You know how to set the stuff off?"

"That's the easy part. It's *not* setting it off that can be a problem."

"Volatile?"

"Very—but no worse than your average Mortal Sin, and I've experience in handling them. Am I to understand that you want me to blow up the *Goose* while you go off, incognito?"

"No, just in disguise. First we drop Elissa and Celia off in Key West. They're the only two left of the women. Then we head to Tortuga. I give the crew leave, all but Luke, my number two. Then you attack."

"How?"

"I've got Lafitte's ship in tow. In fact, Luke and I will be aboard that too. You attack, the *Goose* blows up right over town so everyone can see it, then you drop us off someplace and get to play the hero."

"Where will you go?"

"I've got an idea, but I'll keep that to myself for now. As for the rest of it, the fewer people who know the better. So keep it all under your hat. No one needs to know but you, me, and Luke. Got it?"

"Of course, Jack."

Dinner in Jack's oak-paneled saloon that evening was subdued. Both Celia and Elissa sensed something was afoot. Elissa tried valiantly to maintain her composure—even making a joke about the need to expect the unexpected—but her eyes, all red and puffy, betrayed her. Celia, the plush redhead I'd spent a night with the summer before, seemed more curious than concerned.

Jack and Elissa left the table early. Then Luke, Jack's chubby first mate, went off to attend to some details. That left Celia, me, and two barely touched bottles of wine.

"Come on." She picked up the wine and led me to the elevator. On the way to her deck, she put her arms around my neck and kissed me. The bottles clanked at my back, and I brought a hand up under her skirt. One can't take a steam-powered elevator without arriving at one's destination a little hot and bothered, but we got off this time thoroughly drenched in perspiration.

Celia had a huge room, and a canopied bed about the size of a circus tent. I couldn't really see the point of it. But unlike during our first night together, when she'd seemed somewhat reserved, she revealed an insatiable hunger for innovation. Positions changed every minute or so, and within a few hours, we'd traversed every square inch of the vast acreage.

She'd had me on the brink five or six times. But no sooner would she than she'd flip me one way or another and have me at work on her. It was a game I enjoyed. However, this night, it went on far too long. My frustration began to weigh heavily, as did she, sitting on my chest.

"Tell me what Jack has planned," she said, breathlessly, and while licking my ear.

"I can't. He made me promise."

She started rubbing her bottom across my midsection and I weakened.

"I... I... Really, I can't. I only barely talked him out of killing me this afternoon."

Rarely am I so resolute. But my resolve was buttressed by the suspicion that once I revealed Jack's plan, she would become so preoccupied with that, I wouldn't get to finish things off anyway. She must have sensed this—or was perhaps anxious for a conclusion herself—for she soon relented.

"I'm surprised you held out," she told me afterward. "And a little chagrined—my charms are no match for your fear of Jack."

"Well, I did see a vivid demonstration of his talents earlier today, and a human evisceration is the sort of image that sticks with you."

"Hmm. Then it's lucky for me that I have talents as well."

I'd been resting comfortably, with her head on my chest—but then quite suddenly she had both hands under my arms. She was tickling me. And indeed, she was quite good at it. Within a minute, I'd told her Jack's entire plan.

"I assumed it was something like that. Oh, well. I think we were all a little bored with the game."

"Even Elissa?"

"Yes, even her."

"All right, I told you. Now you tell me Jack's other secret."

"Jack's other secret?" She was playing dumb.

"His secret in bed."

She demurred. So now I took up the tickling. Ultimately, she gave in. But what she told me seemed too fantastic to be believed, and I dare not repeat it lest I lose your confidence—or what little I have of it.

The next morning, we arrived in Havana and Jack and I went off to Cecil's Bar. It being before ten, there were only ten or fifteen barflies in attendance. One of whom was Kelso.

"Good God. You two are connected?" he asked.

"Yeah," Jack told him. "He's helpin' me with that little project I mentioned."

We went to the dark corner which counted as Kelso's office.

"Did you get it?"

"Yes, I got it." Kelso reached under his shirt and carefully took out a small bottle he'd been wearing on a string about his neck.

"Why don't *you* carry it?" Jack more told than asked me.

I gingerly put the string around my own neck and slid the bottle beneath my shirt.

"How about that investment you were going to make for me?" Jack asked.

"For each of you. Step one has been completed. I go back in a week and reap the profits. I'll deposit the sums in a New York bank in your names."

"How much will we clear?"

"Two, three hundred percent. Not bad, eh?"

"It will do," Jack said without much enthusiasm.

"How about that package I gave you to deliver?" I asked.

"I'll drop that off on my next trip."

"Hey," Jack interjected. "Seein' how you got this way of procurin' things, you ever come across a perfume called... What was it again?"

"*Deux nuits d'excès*," I told Kelso. "You may remember, I mentioned it to you before."

"Yes, and I must thank you for it." He laughed. "But it comes a good deal dearer than that explosive."

"How dear?" Jack asked.

"Five thousand a bottle."

The figure he named sounded so ridiculous I laughed. But not Jack.

"Sold. You can deduct it from my share."

"You understand, it's only effective with any one woman for just two nights," Kelso cautioned him.

"Still must come in pretty handy."

"Oh, it does.... Yes, it does."

"How soon can I get it?"

Kelso removed a second string from around his neck, this one holding a small vial. Jack reached for it. But Kelso pulled it away.

"Cash on delivery, I'm afraid."

Jack pulled out a fat roll of hundred-dollar bills, then counted out fifty of them.

The sale completed, they shared a round of drinks. Jack had insisted I forgo liquor for fear it would leave me unsteady on my feet. But once he realized my own fear had left me quite literally quaking in my boots, he took the opposite approach. We eventually stumbled out having temporarily forgotten all about the explosive.

Late that afternoon, we dropped Celia and Elissa off in Key West. Apparently, Jack had no intention of using the perfume on them. There were good-byes all around, then Jack and Elissa went off alone for a few minutes.

"I doubt we'll ever see each other again," Celia said to me.

"Who knows? Any idea where you'll be going?"

"I'll stick with Elissa. She wants to head up north where her people are. A town called Carthage, in New York. Ever hear of it?"

"Not that I recall." I had, in fact. It was a place Jack visited in *The Circensiad*. And there he'd met a girl named Elissa.... But it would have been far too difficult to explain all that in the brief time left.

On the way back to the *Goose*, Jack told me he'd given Elissa a letter explaining everything. "She promised not to open it until tomorrow. Think she'll wait?"

"Doesn't matter. I'm afraid Celia wheedled it out of me last night. She's probably telling Elissa right now. Sorry, Jack."

"She tickled ya, didn't she?"

"Yes, she did.... Say, Jack. One hates to appear mercenary, but those hundreds you flashed this morning in Havana—do you think you could spare a couple?"

"What? Ain't the glory of killin' Jack Tigue enough?" He laughed as he peeled off two bills—but then held them away. "Hey, this perfume. You ever try it on Aggie?"

"Aggie? No, but I did tell her about it, and that alone had a noticeable effect on her. Are you thinking of meeting up with her?"

"Maybe. If I can find her. You said before she headed to the coal fields in Pennsylvania."

"Of course, that was last Christmas. And as you know, she's of a changeable nature. You might check with the New York newspapers, see if she's writing for them."

Only then did he hand over the two hundred.

The remainder of Jack's plan went off without a hitch. After flying to Tortuga, he sent his crew into town and I rigged the explosive. Then we transferred to Lafitte's ship, and, with one well-aimed load of offal from a steam cannon, Jack himself sent *The Buttered Goose* to oblivion. It was a dark, moonless night, so the fiery show was all the more spectacular. But rather than wait for the reviews, we left immediately for Cuba.

Just after sunset of the next day, we brought the ship down in a field twenty miles from the capital.

"This is where we part company," Jack told me. "Just remember, you flew alone. And no one got off the *Goose* alive. Oh, and if you happen to meet up with that supposed wife of yours—well, turnabout is fair play."

"Oh. You must've heard about her and Marpesia...."

His only reply was the cynical half-smile which perennially adorned his face.

"Mere rumors," I assured him.

But he and Luke had already disappeared into the bush.

I left the carcass of Lafitte's ship posthaste—it still contained the remains of him and his crew and the intervening days since their slaughter had not worked to their advantage. One of the many hazards of pirating in a tropical climate.

In Havana, I gave my account to the local press and any correspondents from the mainland I could round up—a pretty simple task for anyone willing to buy rounds at the various bars they frequented. At first they found my story difficult to swallow, even with the free booze. But once the third-party accounts arrived confirming the carnage aboard Lafitte's ship, not to mention the *Goose*'s spectacular demise, they began to see the virtue in my story. Not only did it provide an easily followed narrative explaining events, but acquiring it required no expenditure of effort beyond sitting on a barstool. The word hero was bandied about some. By me, mostly, but someone needed to get the ball rolling.

I spent much of the next few days reveling in my newfound celebrity—a state I'd not experienced since the routing of those circus elephants some years before—but also musing about my future. I considered myself relieved of duty where my wives were concerned. They'd now abandoned me twice and I couldn't drop in on them again without appearing something of a bad penny.

As for my supposed wife, Sesbania, I knew Jack's report that she was pregnant had to be false. If she'd conceived prior to her kidnapping, the child would have been born well before March. And the one night we'd spent together aboard *Lucy* had ended without finality. Besides, wouldn't she have mentioned a small thing like that when she spoke to me from outside my cell window in St. Pierre? No, this was a simple matter between the two of us. And Sesbania had made it amply clear she'd prefer never to see me again.

The obvious course was to sail for Port of Spain, where the amiable Myra would be awaiting me with open arms.

Unfortunately, so was the mad Captain Bonnet, and he not so far away.

III

My abduction had been plotted with a Machiavellian subtlety. It was a Friday night and I'd just spent a long evening singing my praises at the hotel bar. I'd been trying to go light on the female companionship, worried that too-sordid behavior might sully the heroic image I was cultivating. (As it happened, in the Havana of that era opinions on behavior were broad, and my enjoying the company of the curvaceous young wife of a rich old American nearly every afternoon was well within bounds. Her name was Juanita and she came for tea each day at four. At six, the waiter returned and removed the untouched teacart.)

On this particular night, I returned to my suite sometime after two. I was undressing when I heard a woman humming. I opened the door of the bath and there saw a stunningly attractive girl of about twenty. A brunette, with big brown eyes, wonderfully full lips—and not a stitch of clothing.

She smiled at me. Then came at me slowly, swinging her hips as she walked. I don't know why, but as she approached I backed away, until eventually backing onto the bed. In a flash, she was upon me, lavishing me with wet kisses, while her hand massaged me to attention. Then—just as she'd dexterously brought me to the precipice—her appearance changed. And not for the better.

I don't know your opinion of girls with serpents crawling about their hair and blood dripping from their eyes, but my taste very definitely runs in the other direction.

"It is I, Megaera! And I have come for you!"

"Megaera? Have we met before? If so, I'm sure I can explain...."

"Quiet! I am Fury! Punisher of infidelity, broken vows, and theft!"

"Oh. All three? Must keep you busy."

"*Shut up!*"

I did as she asked. God only knows what she looked like when she was angry.

"Come!" She grabbed me by the hair and pulled me along to the balcony just off the sitting room. It was only then that I noticed the wings. "Hang on, or plummet to your death!"

As she lifted off, I clasped her waist. My face was now even with her shapely breasts and I took the opportunity to soften her up with some well-executed tongue work. I thought I heard a few moans of satisfaction, but the drip, drip, drip of blood from her eyes never let up.

By then, I'd remembered that she was one of Bonnet's daughters. He'd actually mentioned her during my last visit with him. Presently, we entered his craft through a large hatchway, where he himself greeted us.

"I'll take care of him, my dear. You better go take a shower."

"Oh. Yes, of course." She'd changed back into her comely self, but now coated in blood.

"Well, we meet again!" he said. "And this time, I'll not be fooled."

"Wouldn't think of trying. Listen, about those collections in New York. It honestly wasn't my fault. I was shanghaied."

"What about impersonating Smedley? And inciting the nymphs to mutiny?"

"Wait a minute—they mutinied *before* liberating me in St. Pierre."

"But only *after* you'd put ideas into their heads! And

what about your wives, stealing my franchise business?"

"I don't see how you can blame me for that."

"A man's responsible for the behavior of his wives!"

"That's rather dated thinking, old man. And certainly doesn't apply to Mortal Sins. After all, you raised them."

"You'll not talk yourself out of it that easily!"

"Talk myself out of what?"

He just laughed. It wasn't a cackle, precisely, but it was most definitely a laugh piratical. He pushed me before him at the point of his cutlass, down one passageway, then up another, and finally locking me in a cabin.

As cells go, it was quite well-appointed—nicely crafted furniture, a comfortable bed, a shelf of books, and even a private bath. There were no windows, only a porthole four inches across, but it seemed airy enough.

Breakfast was served by a berobed maiden of unknown mythical mandate. She had to lean down to slip the tray through the hatch at the bottom of the door. Her robe dipped and I could see two perfect hemispheres.

"Tell me," she said. "Is it true?"

"Is what true?"

"Can you... Can you really..."

Before she could go on, an older woman called her from somewhere behind and she hurried off.

It was that second, older woman who came an hour later for the tray.

"I don't know if you remember me," she began.

"Oh, I do. You're Euphrosyne, aren't you?"

"Yes.... Smedley's wife. We sat next to one another at dinner. The evening before your wedding.... I want you to know, had I realized Father would cheat you like that, I would certainly have warned you."

"Of course. You needn't blame yourself."

"Thank you.... Um, this is rather awkward."

"What exactly?"

"Well, there's a rumor. About you... and, well... It's not something one can speak about, politely. And..."

"And being a Grace you find it impossible to do otherwise?"

"Oh, yes! You're so understanding."

"I try to be. Perhaps if you worded your query obliquely."

"I did think of something. Though perhaps it's a little too oblique...."

"Well, you can give it a try."

"All right. My question is, can you touch the tip of your nose with your tongue?"

"As a matter of fact, I can." We were both leaning down—nearly on the floor. So it made my demonstration doubly difficult. Nonetheless, I complied.

I'm not sure I would have deduced the purpose of her inquiry had not another conversation many years before begun with the exact same question. It was the one with my Latin teacher the day she had me to her house to split firewood....

Euphrosyne smiled in reply, then left with the tray. Much to my disappointment, she didn't return at lunch, nor at supper.

She did, however, sneak in sometime that night. I'd been sleeping soundly and suddenly felt a body next to mine.

"It's me," she said—and those were the only words spoken by either of us that night.

I knew what she was there for and I certainly wasn't going to make her ask twice. I gave her the full treatment.

To keep herself from uttering a sound, she placed my hand in her mouth. She bit down on it once or twice, hard, but mostly she just sucked on it. She was clearly a woman who knew more about giving than receiving, but on this night, I felt she deserved some payback from my side of the equation and I did what I could to even the score. I finally finished inside her, her mouth now occupied with mine.

I fully expected to be leaving the cell with her. What I would do then, I wasn't sure. Just so long as I could find some way of escaping Bonnet and whatever plans he had for me. Unfortunately, not long after giving Euphrosyne her due, I fell into a deep sleep. When I woke, I was alone. I called out in the darkness, but she was gone. All I could do was hope she'd return the next night.

That next day passed slowly. Bonnet's choice of reading material ran a little literary for my liking. An afternoon spent with Plutarch's lives of the Romans and Greeks left me craving something with some spice, say an old issue of Capt. Billy's Whiz Bang. On a positive note, they served filet of sole and a lobster bisque for supper, so by lights out, I felt able and ready for the Grace's second coming.

After a few hours of waiting, I dozed some, and it was during one of these spells that she must have entered. Only it wasn't the fair and ever-congenial Euphrosyne, but her sister, the angry and ever-vengeful Megaera.

"You have committed adultery in the very house of your wives' father!"

Put like that, it did sound rather uncouth of me. But I decided I might as well plead my case. I pointed out that rather than enjoying his hospitality, I was Bonnet's prisoner. And that it was his fault for marrying the poor girl to a selfish bastard like Smedley, which left her, as a woman, unfulfilled.

"Would you really condemn me for bringing your much-trod-upon sister a fleeting hour of pleasure?"

It was only now, when the Fury asked for details, that I realized my death might not be quite so imminent as I feared. I'd piqued her curiosity. And a brief moment later, I was doing likewise to her little demon in the boat.

Through it all, blood dripped from her eyes, and serpents played hide-and-seek in her lush mane. But I did catch hints that she was enjoying herself. Every once in a while her head would swing back and she'd sort of yeeowl like a she-cat in heat. Not normally an attractive sound, but fitting given the present circumstances.

She stopped me short of entering her, perhaps due to some legalistic interpretation of adultery. Instead she set upon me as I had her. She had a remarkable technique, perhaps attributable to the cleft in her tongue—though the queer sensation of serpents skittering about on my belly did put a small crimp in my delight. When I eventually went off, she appeared to find a near equal satisfaction in my completion of the mission, letting out a yeeowl to end all yeeowls.

Then she asked me if I'd learned my lesson, and I assured her I had. It struck me as curious that the punishment she'd dispensed so closely resembled the crime, but I suppose the pagans are no better at overcoming hypocrisy than the monotheists.

With her now changed back to her normal self, the two of us shared a shower—an obligatory coda given the quantity of blood she'd loosed. She snuck off while I was still drying myself. But not before I advised her to have some beef liver for breakfast. She definitely needed to replenish her iron if she was going to carry on like that.

Rather than return to the sticky bed, I spent the rest of the night in a not very comfortable chair.

I awoke the next morning feeling myself lucky to be alive. And all the more so when I learned it was the day the bed linen was changed—but then appreciably less so when Bonnet dropped by to disclose that he'd arranged to barter me.

Chapter 10.

Telling Tales

Bonnet left me the afternoon to ponder what precise calamity lay in store. However, his use of the word barter had come as a small relief, as I'd feared something along the lines of keelhauling... or walking the plank... or, if he was in a hurry, beheading.

But what did he expect to trade me for, so many head of sheep? With both the Cyclops and the Lafittes residing in the past tense, my market value should have taken a nose dive. Especially since Marpesia had refocused her wrath on Jack. If anything, I would have expected her to feel some indebtedness for my having (apparently) rid the world of her nemesis.

I was still trying to calculate my worth in livestock when several burly nymphs arrived. They claimed to be dryads, but were built more like lumberjacks. I tried working my charm on their apparent leader and she nearly broke my jaw with a well-placed jab.

They led me to an open hatch, from which a midair gangway had been strung between Bonnet's craft and another, much larger one. It was *The Midnight Sun,* and walking across toward us was the one item I *did* approximate in value: me. Or, at least, my doppelganger, Smedley.

Could it be that Marpesia, having heard of my dispatching of Jack and subsequent capture by Bonnet, agreed to this exchange in order to save my life and thereby repay the debt? Frankly, the odds of that were infinitesimally small. But in times of desperation, one must grasp at whatever straws present themselves. And this thin reed of hope was all that kept me from sliding into the black abyss of despair.

Unfortunately, the odds lengthened even further when Smedley came nearer into view. He now looked an elder version of me—I'd have guessed fifty if a day. His hair had grayed and lines creased his face. As he passed, he looked at me wearily. Then smiled as if mildly amused.

"Be careful what you wish for," he said.

I wanted to ask him to elaborate, but by then the wood-chopping nymphs were prodding me with their peavies. I considered taking a swan dive into the sea below. In the early-evening sun, it looked not nearly as dark as the black abyss of despair I was headed for. But I reckoned our altitude as at least a thousand feet and my chances of survival as nil.

On the far side, I was greeted by several burly Amazons armed with javelins. I made a little joke about the symmetry the two parties of tormentors presented, but I laughed alone. And not for long. A javelin stuck in one's flank makes mirth problematic; three together quite effectively put the kibosh on thoughts of merriment altogether.

They herded me from one wide passageway to another. Then the forewoman knocked on an imposing door.

"Enter," came a distant reply.

We did so, then needed to walk another hundred feet to reach the huge desk where Marpesia was at work. The room was only slightly larger than your average-size concert hall, but the sparse furnishings made it seem even larger. There were all sorts of correspondence and ledgers stacked before the Amazon queen, and she was busily checking figures in one of the account books. I never would have suspected being an Amazon pirate queen involved so much paperwork.

Her jet-black hair was pinned up in the back, but only to shorten its length—the last of it falling to her shoulders rather than the small of her back. Atop the mane sat a tiara, tastefully compact in size and bejeweled with admirable restraint. Of her peacock-blue gown, I could see only the upper third—just enough to appreciate the way it combined the majestic with the practical. It was of some linen-like fabric, suitable to the warm climate, but incorporating sufficient gilt embroidery to imbue its wearer with a regal air. Taken together, it was the sort of casual costume the Queen of Sheba might wear about the palace on days when only minor aristocrats were expected.

No one said a word until Marpesia finished her calculations and closed the book. Then she slowly lifted her gaze to me.

"So, we meet again."

"Yes. I do hope things are well with you." Her only reply to that was to twist her lips. Not a good sign, I thought. "By the way, just in case you haven't seen a newspaper, I thought you might be relieved to learn I destroyed that villain, Jack Tigue."

"Yes, I heard of your theatrics. I'm surprised you haven't mounted his head on a pole."

"I don't believe there was anything left larger than an ear, and that seemed hardly worth the trouble. Apparently, he'd been carrying some sort of high-explosive."

"How incautious of him.... And how lucky for you."

"Yes, it was rather lucky."

"But now, unfortunately, your luck has changed...."

"Has it?"

"Perhaps not—assuming you have on a parachute."

"Parachute? I'm afraid my invitation made no mention of proper attire."

"Oh, how regrettable. A fall from ten thousand feet is so rarely survived without one. I must have a word with my stationer. Now, if you are done with the drollery, we might get down to the matter at hand."

"Which matter, specifically?"

"I know now that Eugenia was not aboard Tigue's ship."

"No—definitely not. She was safely away. I made sure of that before even considering my assault."

"Yes, I know all about your involvement. You see, what I've heard—only recently, and from a very reliable source—is that she left his ship months ago in Port Royal, and afterward traveled from that town in your company."

"Well, you certainly are well informed."

"Put an end to your obfuscation, or you'll find yourself among the sharks already circling below us. I want to know where she is, and I want to know now."

I thought she'd gone a little too far by claiming an intimate knowledge of these sharks' current position and course. However, later I learned that the Amazons dumped a daily ration of animal parts into the sea for the sole purpose of keeping the razor-toothed fish in attendance. The species to which these animals belonged, my confidante told me, varied, but consisted mainly of those the Amazons found not to their taste. Then, after a long pause, she added that they were not, after all, cannibals. Pirate girls, by and large, share a very strange sense of humor.

Had I known all that at the time, I might have been more forthcoming. As it was, I told Marpesia that Eugenia had instructed me not to reveal her plans. "She mentioned you specifically."

"*Why?*"

"Why? Well... no idea, really. She just told me to be sure not to tell either you or Jack."

"I see. But knowing her—as we both do—we might well suppose she would never hold you to that promise if you were... under duress."

"Under duress?"

"*Painful* duress."

Her meaning was clear enough, and came with a bit more menace than the words alone convey. The phrase "as we both do" encompassed long pauses between words. I deduced from this that the thought did not please her. She brightened appreciably, however, when clarifying the nature of my duress. It was that lingering look of satisfaction, combined with the javelin point planted firmly in my flank, which effected my capitulation.

"I suppose you're right. Eugenia is nothing if not forgiving. All right, I dropped her off in Martinique."

"Why Martinique?"

"She planned on taking an airship to Marseilles."

"Why would she want to go to Marseilles?"

"She wanted to go to France. I think Marseilles just happened to be where the airship landed."

"To have the baby...."

"Yes, that's right." Until then, it wasn't clear she knew about Eugenia's pregnancy. But I suppose whoever had spied on us in Port Royal could hardly have missed the fact. I tried to change the subject. "Lovely country,

France. We visited it just last year. Sesbania and I. Or, should I say, Orithyia."

"Unless you're anxious to make the acquaintance of those sharks, you should stick to the subject at hand. I'm going to ask this question just once. Who is the father of that baby?"

"Jack, of course." There were only two people capable of contradicting me, and they were neither available nor so inclined. Besides, the reward for truth telling on this occasion was unlikely to differ in any substantive way from the penalty for prevaricating. Either way, the sharks would have their supper. "He picked her up in Nassau last summer. Perhaps you remember?"

"Oh, I remember. *And* I remember your trial—and all that emerged in the testimony there. Every detail is still quite fresh in my mind. So too is a conversation I had with a certain member of the hotel's staff."

Damn that chambermaid!

"Look, you can ask Eugenia herself when you see her."

"I will. When I see her. But that will be too late for you. You see, there's also the matter of that ransom notice you had published."

"Oh, the ransom notice. Well, the way that came about is really rather silly...."

"I somehow doubt we'll see eye to eye on that point. But regardless, you'd best save it for your trial."

"Trial?"

"Yes, you heard correctly. Though if you'd prefer to plead guilty, throw yourself on the mercy of the court, and take what comes—that option is always available."

"No, no. A trial will do quite nicely."

"Yes, I thought you might think so. Take him away."

She turned her attention back to her paperwork and my escort prodded me out of the room and along a couple more passageways. The interview had not gone as well as I'd hoped. That thin reed I'd been grasping onto proved far too fragile a metaphor to prevent my descent into that of the black abyss.

The cell they brought me to was larger than the one I'd had aboard Bonnet's ship, but not nearly so comfortably furnished. The bed seemed to consist of a plank with a single sheet and no pillow whatsoever.

"If you make any attempt to escape, our orders are to kill you on the spot. If you show even the slightest inclination to rebel, we are to kill you on the spot. Or, should you neglect your hygiene, and begin to smell disagreeable..."

"Kill me on the spot?"

"If not sooner. All clear?"

"Yes, I think I've got it. Wash twice daily, and betweentimes, cower in fear."

"Precisely."

"I have just one small request. I wonder if you could get word to Sesbania—I mean, Orithyia—that I'm aboard and would beseech an audience, involving whatever displays of obsequiousness protocol demands."

"Oh, she'll be coming, all right. And when she does, I suggest you spare her your feigned servility. Groveling will get you nowhere. You really are an unctuous little toady, aren't you?"

She didn't wait for my riposte—which was just as well, since repartee with an armed adversary has rarely turned out well for me. The moment they locked the door, I ran through her list of proscriptions. It had been a warm, humid day, and that—combined with all the prodding, threats, and foreshadowing of my impending doom—had left me in a state a stickler for hygiene might find objectionable.

I went into the conveniently attached bathroom. This too was commodious, as was the tub. But the water, like the Amazons themselves, ran only cold.

II

About three hours later, I was brought supper. The food was actually quite good, but the portions petite in the extreme. I assumed I'd been placed on half rations, because no pirates—male or female—could maraud at their best on three measly medallions of pork tenderloin and a fruit cup. Whatever his faults, the mad Captain Bonnet knew how to put on a meal The grub was both plentiful and delectable, and his master chef a veritable goddess of the hearth. (One of his in-laws, I believe—a woman named Hestia.)

A shelf of books hung above my plank bed, and after my meal I dipped into one. It was called *The Awakening* and belonged to that category of novel which explores the myriad ways wives find marriage a dissatisfying slog. Pretty dull stuff. I skipped to the end just to see if anything of consequence came about, only to find the heroine working hard to drown herself. Upon closer examination I realized the whole shelf was devoted to the unhappy-marriage genre. Next in line was *Madame Bovary*, and at the far end, the Oedipus cycle—the last word in unhappy marriages. I gathered the library had been chosen with a particular line of argument in mind.

"Are you decent?" a familiar voice called from outside.

It was Sesbania, and I took it for granted her question was a loaded one.

"As pure as the day I was born," I told her.

"Then throw on some clothes."

"It's only my soul which is bared."

She unlocked the door and came in. "I'd be careful on that front if I were you."

I rose and approached her, but she held up her hand and waved me off.

"That wouldn't be appropriate, under the circumstances."

She looked little changed from when I'd last seen her the summer before. She may have put on a few pounds, but was definitely not with child. Perhaps the fare was more plentiful in the officers' mess. For a moment, I feared she'd shaved off her tresses. But once she doffed the tricorne set jauntily upon her head, her chestnut mane fell loose about her shoulders. And though garbed in the regulation pirate-girl costume of battered blouse and tattered knee britches, as always with her, she wore it to advantage.

"You're looking well," I told her. "Spectacularly well, considering...."

"Considering what?" She looked at me with genuine curiosity.

"Well, your travails...."

"Oh, yes. My travails. I forgot about those. It seems so long ago. And what about you? You're looking... *well...*"

"A little worse for the wear?"

"Yes, I'm afraid so. You've had a taxing time, haven't you?"

"To say the least. Five months imprisoned, shoveling offal. Then two bouts as galley slave aboard Jean Lafitte's blood-sodden airship."

"I was speaking of your seven wives. And the girl who so easily misled you into thinking she was me."

"Not easily. She'd been put up to it by a newspaper-woman with a perverse sense of humor. She even knew about my scar!"

"And *how* did she learn of that?"

"That reporter told her."

"And how did *she* know of it?"

"Ah. She spied on me through a peephole."

"A peephole? How quaint. Is this the same woman you vacationed with in Tortuga last winter?"

"I'd hardly call that a vacation. I was evading the fiendish Cyclops, La Baza—whom, I'll have you know, I have since vanquished."

"Have you, now? Was that when you'd set up house with the barkeep in Port of Spain?"

"Immediately before that. And it's not as if I'm some sort of serial Lothario by choice. Women have a habit of abandoning me."

"How very surprising. But I'm not sure that argument will serve you well in court."

"In court? You mean this trial Marpesia has planned?"

"Yes, that's the one."

"I assume it will be before a jury of my peers. After all, the Bill of Rights guarantees..."

"I wouldn't bring up rights of any sort if I were you. And I fail to see what advantage you'd gain from a jury of your peers: con men, adulterers, bigamists, thieves... men easily corruptible and completely lacking in fealty...."

Her naïveté surprised me. Apparently, she'd never found it necessary to suborn a jury.

"You're laying it on a bit thick, aren't you? People who live in glass houses...."

"What are you implying?"

"I'm afraid your affair with Marpesia has become grist for the trans-Caribbean gossip mill."

"Oh. Well, I don't see what bearing that has on the matter. Technically, you can't really call it adultery."

"Well, you can scarcely accuse me of it either. We were never married. And as to the charge of bigamy, I was merely following the religious precepts of my wives— hardly a condemnable act."

"If you claim to have been legally bound to them, I don't see how you can evade the charge of adultery."

"*They* abandoned *me!* Twice."

"Yes. I remember now hearing of that first occasion. That was when you arranged to bunk with that woman in Nassau."

"In fact, we never bunked together. If you're so well informed, you should remember that I was staying in a hotel when I was arrested."

Needless to say, I immediately regretted opening that can of worms. Her expression, which had been one of vague disgust and annoyance, became one of acute repugnance.

"Oh, you're lucky winged Fury doesn't swoop down and wreak her vengeance!"

"You know Megaera? Frankly, her bark is worse than her bite. In fact, I don't remember her biting—"

"*What?*"

"Sorry, just a recurring nightmare of mine."

"As well it should be!"

"Listen, Sesbania, I'm truly sorry if I've offended you. I had hoped..."

"Hoped to win me over with lies, and false flattery, just like all the others?"

"Well, it worked the first time...."

I don't think she appreciated my little joke. It looked for a moment as if blood might spurt from her eyes like the Fury's.

"Please spare me your feeble attempts at wit. If you have any interest in making it through this ordeal, I suggest we keep our business to the matter at hand—your trial."

"Will you be playing a part?"

"Oh, yes. I'm the counsel for the defense."

"How providential."

"We'll see about that."

There was a knock at the door. Sesbania answered it and exchanged whispers with someone in the hall. And then a third voice joined in—much louder than the other two. When Sesbania returned, she was carrying a baby. A baby with a grievance.

"Sit down," she told me. "And hold her while I prepare her supper."

I did as she instructed and she placed the erupting bundle in my lap. Then she sat beside me and brought forth a nipple—quite easily done, as brevity is the very soul of pirate-girl fashion.

"Aren't you going to greet your daughter?"

"My daughter?"

She looked at me blankly for a moment—Sesbania, I mean. The baby wasn't looking at anything, her eyes closed so she could concentrate on shrieking.

"I named her Elizabeth. Liz. After a friend.

"You mean, Liz Rutledge—aka Antiope?"

"Yes. I couldn't bring myself to put Antiope on the birth certificate, but around the house.... Better hand her back before she loses her temper."

I watched the child sup and all thoughts of my trial—beyond a nebulous notion of calamity—drifted from my mind.

"How old is she?" I asked. It was just an offhand remark, but Sesbania looked me in the eye before replying.

"Two months. It had to be that one night we spent together on the way to Nassau."

"Yes, it had to be."

"You don't look very pleased."

"Well, I will be as soon as I get over the shock. I imagine raising pirate girls is no easy task."

We exchanged smiles, then sat silently until baby Liz had her fill.

"Now I must be going. I'll be back in the morning to start planning our case."

"OK. I'm glad."

"About?"

"Oh, all of it—the baby, that you're defending me...."

"I'll do what I can, Pluribus. But I'm no miracle worker. Good-bye."

I'd always thought one of a defense attorney's principal tasks was to cheer the client with optimistic platitudes. Sesbania would need to work on her patter if she were to make a career of it. I did, however, take some heart in the fact my child's mother would be defending me. She had a vested interest in my survival. Of course, whether that was enough to offset all the lingering resentments remained to be seen.

It also assumed she really believed me to be the father. The prime candidate in my book was Smedley. He'd been brought aboard as me, and no doubt Sesbania had found a way of joining him. Though he would have asserted his true identity under Marpesia's interrogation, if Sesbania had crawled into bed beside him, calling him Pluribus, he'd surely have played along.

The picture I'd painted wasn't a pleasant one. To comfort myself, I spent the rest of the evening reading *Oedipus Rex*. Nothing like a Greek tragedy to put one's familial complications in perspective.

III

Sesbania came by just as I finished my breakfast—a bowl of yogurt with sliced strawberries, a piece of coarse toast, and tea. Coffee, bacon, and eggs, I was told, were unavailable. My guard suggested I might lodge a protest with the cook.

"Bertha's her name—she's usually butchering lunch about now. Shall I tell her you'd like a chat?"

I demurred. Pirate cooks wielding cleavers rarely welcome criticism, no matter how constructive.

Once we were left alone, Sesbania took up her pen.

"You'll need to tell me everything that's happened since that night aboard the *Paris*."

"Everything?"

"Of course. I have to be prepared for whatever Marpesia throws at us. She's a very cunning adversary."

"Is that what won you over?"

"*What?*"

"Sorry. Mere curiosity."

"Look, Pluribus, that first night I was drugged!"

"*Deux nuits d'excès.*"

"Yes! Well, you can't imagine what it's like...."

"And the second night goes without saying...."

"Exactly. And after that... well."

"Well, indeed."

"Look, just remember, *you're* the one on trial. Now, that night, when the airship arrived, what were you doing up on the boat deck?"

"Let's see. There had been some talk of keelhauling, but eventually the boys settled on having me walk the plank."

"*What?*"

She was laughing. And all through the well-edited narrative of those initial episodes (friendly colleens, obliging hookers, attentive nurses, and inhibited Norse-women all went unmentioned), she went on laughing. Right up until the point where Emmie confirmed my suspicions about steam-powered airships and Amazon pirates.

"Are you saying your cousin Emmie is somehow aware of this parallel world?"

"Most definitely. You've read her books—don't you remember Jack Tigue, and Eugenia Biddle?"

"I thought the names sounded familiar, but assumed it was just an odd coincidence. So has your cousin traveled here as well?"

"No, she's received her briefings via some inter-world delivery service—if you believe her."

"And if you don't?"

"Well, it's generally been assumed she made the whole thing up. In which case, we're currently residing in a world of her making."

"That's ridiculous!"

"So one would hope. But it would account for the distorted geography. Did you know that here, Madagascar is in the Caribbean, Nova Scotia in the South Pacific, and Prince Edward Island a mere myth?"

"How odd. Just out of curiosity, where is Madagascar normally?"

"The Indian Ocean, off of Africa."

"Oh, yes.... You know, Marpesia assumes the real world—or the one we consider real—is the copy and this the original."

"What else would she think?"

"I don't suppose it makes much difference in the end.... Well, let's get on with your story."

I told her of our encounter with the hurricane, Aggie's stowing away, and my first jailing in Nassau. Then on to Tortuga (sans Clarisse), meeting Jack, and the unpleasantness at the Lafittes' base in Barataria.

"You see, everyone I spoke with thought Jean Lafitte the likely abductor of women from a steamship. Then at Barataria, his brother Pierre led me to believe you were being auctioned up in St. Pierre."

"But he was talking of my doppelganger."

"Yes." I skipped my abandonment of Jack, and the interlude on the Delaware River, but couldn't avoid telling her of my run-in with mad Captain Bonnet.

"So you're saying you had to marry these seven daughters to get the liquor back with which you planned to bid on me? That's a little tortuous, isn't it?"

"Do you honestly think I would marry the Mortal Sins of Wrath, Pride, Envy, Avarice, and Sloth if I wasn't forced into the match?"

"Sloth if she was attractive, and Avarice almost certainly. Besides, you left out the other two."

"Clio and Melpomene. Can you even conceive what it's like to spend time with the Muse of tragic poetry? The wailing just never ends."

"And Clio?"

"Bookish. The most agreeable of the lot, but that's not saying much. Anyway, I had no choice. Smedley was as sly as his father-in-law." I watched her face at mention of the name, but she betrayed no particular interest. "What did you think of him? Smedley, I mean."

"Think of him?"

"Well, when he first came aboard, you'd been led to believe he was me."

"Yes. Marpesia was very angry when she learned he was an impostor. I had hoped to persuade her that you had some explanation, for that ransom note, and... so on.... She sent me to confirm your identity. Of course, I knew at once he wasn't you."

"How?"

"Most obviously because *he* didn't recognize *me*. But then I thought, would Pluribus be so devious that he'd pretend not to know me simply to avoid Marpesia's wrath? So I had him show me his shin—no scar."

"Then why did Marpesia keep him aboard for so long?"

"Well, at first she disbelieved me. She thought I was conspiring with you to save your life."

"How did you convince her otherwise?"

"It took some... cajoling.... And I recounted some of the less savory episodes from your past, to explain why my attachment to you was so tentative."

"What about after that? She could have at least ransomed him to Bonnet."

"Well, by then, there was a faction who'd decided he

could be made use of. Apparently—at least, so it was reported—he could maintain a... let us say, a firmness of purpose, for far longer than normal men. I guess in that way, you two are really quite easily distinguished...."

I didn't share her laugh.

"So he was used to service the crew?"

"Just a small faction. A small, but spirited, faction. At first, he was enthusiastic. But I suspect that eventually their spiritedness got the better of his enthusiasm—but we should get back to your story. What happened in St. Pierre?"

I told her. Then told her about my marriages, including the various consummations (she insisted on details and she, by and large, got them), and my second time out on a plank. And, since she already knew about them, the episodes involving Clem, Gertie, Aggie, and Myra. But about Eugenia, I kept mum.

I didn't finish until almost two, and when I did, the three of us had a late lunch. From the looks of it, baby Liz was as famished as I was.

The meal over, Sesbania said she needed all the time left to prepare for the trial.

"It's scheduled to begin at ten tomorrow morning. I'll be by to pick you up at quarter of."

"All right. But in the meantime, could you send over something to read? The selection here seems designed to depress."

"Oh," she said, her eyes running along the shelf. "Well, you see, this room is usually used as part of Marpesia's reeducation program."

"Reeducation program?"

"Yes. Say you have a crew member who continues to harbor romantic ideas about marriage. Stick her in here

211

for a week or two, with nothing to do but read, and she'll soon be having second thoughts. Next, you place her in a cabin with all the amenities—big, soft bed, plenty to eat, several bottles of wine, provocative murals covering walls and ceilings, and a library where men feature not at all."

"I wouldn't think people so easily swayed, given the matter involves biology as much as intellect."

"It's one of Marpesia's weak points. She can't imagine how anyone would feel differently about marriage. She refers to wives as little more than walking sheaths, and always in the Latin. One must admit, of course, in a broad political sense, her argument is unassailable."

"In a broad political sense?"

"If not morally and ethically. Plus, those murals... Well, they really set a girl to thinking. I'll send over a volume of Sappho and friends. Until morning."

No sooner had she and the baby left than my mind raced back to Smedley. I felt sure she'd been holding something back. Something she'd prefer to forget about. And my jealousy rivaled my curiosity. But if I were to probe the subject further, she might inquire about *my* night with Eugenia. Better we both adopt a forgiving attitude. After all, as Jack had said, turnabout is fair play.

I fell asleep reading the book she sent over, a compendium of Greek love poems. Not my cup of tea normally, but the imagery gave me something to think about. I was in the throes of a pretty randy dream when I was awoken by five well-proportioned females.

Unfortunately, these were not the diaphanous-robed maidens of my revelry, but another squad of javelin-wielding Amazons.

"Get up! Your time has come!" the apparent sergeant of the guard shouted.

"Looks still dark out. I thought the trial was on for ten o'clock."

"Well, it's your lucky night. Marpesia has decided to speed things up!" She cackled, then the others followed her lead.

"I'm all for efficiency, but isn't that taking things a little far?"

Apparently, she thought not. They dragged me out of bed wearing just the nightshirt I'd been provided and prodded me through several long corridors. Ultimately, we came to a door labeled Drying Room. There was also a paper sign tacked to the door. While we awaited a response to the sergeant's knock, I read it:

Notice: Absolutely no wash is to be hung on evenings prior to executions. Failure to abide by this edict will result in said wash being thrown into the sea. You have been warned!

As it seemed unlikely I'd been brought there to hang laundry, I took the warning as an omen of bad tidings.

The room was large and airy, with hatchways on either side providing for cross-ventilation. Near one of the hatchways, a knot of women had gathered. Marpesia, per usual, towered above the others. She was draped in black, and her tiara replaced by a little cap of the same color.

"You've been charged with and convicted of being a typical male ass. Your punishment is to walk the plank!"

"What about my trial?"

"Yes, your trial. Pity you won't be alive to participate. Care to guess the outcome?"

"No, no. I'm nothing if not patient."

"Laugh now—for in a minute, nothing is what will be left of you! Those poor sharks haven't been fed in three days." She turned to the sergeant of the guard. "All right, let's get on with it."

Only then did I see Sesbania among the spectators. She was holding the baby.

"Say good-bye to your papa, Liz."

She waved the baby's hand for her and smiled an enigmatic smile. Then the baby smiled the exact same enigmatic smile. I smiled back, for clearly the whole thing had to be a joke.

Or so I assumed—right up until the point where the javelin-wielders had me at the very end of the plank. It was a windy night, and I took some small comfort in the fact I could hear the waves below. We must not have been more than fifty or sixty feet up. A survivable drop, given the right conditions. The first of those conditions being a complete absence of ravenous sharks.

"Now!" Marpesia commanded, and suddenly both the plank and I were in free fall.

If I could get ahold of the plank and keep myself out of the water, I thought, I might have a chance. Not an easy task given the weather. Even less so once the plank came down on the crown of my head just as I entered the drink.

It didn't knock me out, fortunately. However, no matter how hard I tried, I couldn't arrest my descent. Deeper and deeper I went, encountering all manner of sea creatures: octopi, giant squids, gliding rays, and other strange fish in their dozens—but no man-eaters among them. Even more miraculously, I seemed in no danger of drowning.

Then, all at once, they were upon me. Not sharks, but mermaids—a whole comely school of them. They petted and caressed, kissed and stroked me. However, when I tried doing likewise to any of them, they pulled away.

As they swam about me, I spotted one the spitting image of Sesbania—from the waist up, of course. She was a little more receptive, and allowed me to touch her. I was, naturally, anxious to answer the age-old riddle: where does a mermaid hide her... you know... secret parts? A visual survey afforded me no comfort, for I could discern no solution to the mystery.

Had I in fact drowned, and was this to be my own personal Hell? To spend all of eternity surrounded by inviting maidens—and no way to express my admiration?

I simply had to get to the bottom of the conundrum and it could only be done by way of one of theirs. I latched onto fish-tailed Sesbania and initiated a thorough exploration.

Her response was to slap me hard across the face.

CHAPTER 11.

JUST DESERTS

"Damn it, Pluribus, wake up!"

Suddenly, I was back in bed, with Sesbania leaning over me and my right hand doing reconnaissance under her judicial robes.

"*And get your paw off of me!*"

"Sorry. I must have been having a dream."

"I think I can guess what it involved.... You'd better hurry up and get ready, or we'll be late."

"Yes, I wouldn't want to miss my execution."

"No need to be sarcastic. You'll have your day in court—first."

While I dressed, I told her of my nightmare. Her only response was to ask me what she had worn to the execution.

"A sort of black gown, I think."

"The one with the high collar?"

"As a matter of fact, I think it did have a high collar."

"Yes, that will be perfect."

The chief difficulty in deciphering the pirate-girl sensibility is that it combines a wicked sense of humor with a jocular sense of wickedness. Like a mouse cornered by a cat, her victim knows only that he's being toyed with. How the game will end is entirely up to the cat.

She escorted me to the place of trial and at precisely ten o'clock Marpesia entered, dressed in smartly cut magenta robes. She crossed the room with the bearing of a monarch.

Whether she could actually lay claim to the title of

Amazon queen, I can't say. But she did look the part. Particularly when her lips were twisted into a contemptuous sneer as they were just then. Upon her head, she wore a different bejeweled tiara—this one easily twice the size of the one she'd sported the day before. That it wasn't the black cap of condemnation came as a relief. Nonetheless, her attitude looked to be anything but forgiving. She gaveled the court to order with such force that the tomahawk she used as gavel became hopelessly embedded in the judicial bench.

"Clerk of the Court, you may begin."

One of the underlings near the front rose and cleared her throat.

"The sole case today is *The People versus E. Pluribus Van Slyke*. The accused is charged with forty-nine counts of fraud, seventeen counts of theft, six counts of bigamy, a gross of adultery, two counts of kidnapping, and acts of deceit too numerous to be tallied.... Oh, and he killed some people."

"Any women among them?"

The clerk examined her paperwork. "No... apparently not."

"Then you may strike those charges. How does the defendant plead?"

Sesbania answered for me. "We would like to reserve our plea for the moment."

"Then enter a plea of not guilty into the record—as absurd as it is. Prosecutor, you may begin."

"Just look at the knave, Your Honor. Have you ever seen such a sorry specimen? Well, what more needs to be said? The prosecution rests."

"Good. I hope the defense will be equally alacritous. I have a working lunch scheduled *and* a meeting of the

Committee on Castration and Impalement. Be nice if we could work both in."

I hoped by both she meant the lunch and the meeting. But from the way she was grinning at me, I suspected otherwise.

"Your Honor, I call as my first and only witness, the defendant."

"Good. This should be fun."

I took the stand and Sesbania had me give a synopsis of my saga up until my initial escape from jail in Nassau. The judge looked alternately bored and incredulous—but always annoyed.

"Next, you took command of the airship *Lucy's Revenge*, and then traveled to Tortuga. Isn't that right?" Sesbania asked.

"Yes. And then from there up to Barataria, where I hoped to reunite with you."

"Yes, but before leaving Tortuga, did you not share a dinner with—*and* sample the favors of—a demonstrative barkeep named Clarisse?"

How in God's name had she heard about Clarisse?

"Well... The situation was a perilous one, and she's a difficult woman to deny."

"Is she, now?"

Something had gone amiss. Sesbania was sounding unmistakably prosecutorial.

"Yes. And anyway, we never exactly finished the... meal."

"*Oh, please!*" the judge interjected. Her contemptuous sneer had now all but eclipsed her remaining features.

"You didn't find me in Barataria, so you went on from there," Sesbania continued.

"Yes. Up to St. Pierre, where I was told you were to be auctioned by the fiend Jean Lafitte."

"I think you skipped a couple episodes the court may be interested in."

"Well, I was attacked on the way to Barataria by the devilishly mad Captain Bonnet."

"Yes, but even well before that. You had some sort of engine trouble over Pennsylvania, and made an unscheduled stop in Port Jervis for repairs. There you met a young and innocent librarian and secreted her aboard your airship. A virgin."

I'd been betrayed by a spy, all right. But why was Sesbania making things worse for me?

"She was young, but believe me, not nearly so innocent as you've been misled to believe. And I didn't secret her aboard. We were having a sort of impromptu carnival to raise money for repairs. And she asked to see the crow's nest."

"*Oh, did she?*" Those words were uttered by both Sesbania and the judge simultaneously, and in an identical tone.

"Yes! And she was quite insistent that I..."

"Ruin her?"

"Well, that wasn't her choice of words, but essentially, yes."

The courtroom erupted into a sea of silent scornful sneers and furrowed brows.

Describing how the polygamous marriage came about was painful in the extreme, especially when I let slip that I'd originally arranged to take Erato as part of my allotment.

"That slut?" the stenographer inquired rhetorically.

I had faith I'd at least be acquitted of the kidnapping

charges. I assumed one count involved Eugenia and the ill-conceived ransom note. But I couldn't imagine who the other involved.

As it turned out, it was their very own Antiope.

"But she defected!" I protested. "You were there yourself, Your Honor."

"It would be inappropriate for me to testify. The law demands that I remain impartial."

"Thank you, Your Honor," Sesbania groveled. "The defense appreciates your principled attitude in the matter."

It was an utter mockery. I had fairer trials in Gertie's kangaroo court.

When we eventually got to the night with Eugenia in Nassau, Marpesia took it upon herself to question me.

"Now, I will ask this one last time. Is there even the remotest possibility you are the father of her child?"

"No, Your Honor, I swear on my mother's grave!" Not that I had any idea whether she was dead or alive.

She stared at me for ten full seconds. And sneered too, of course.

"On this one point, the court accepts your testimony—but only because the alternative is simply too repugnant to be entertained."

"Your Honor is too kind." In a courtroom like hers, one must take one's victories as they come.

No one seemed particularly interested in the remainder of my tale. About twelve thirty, Marpesia looked up at the clock.

"Enough," she said. "Bring on the brat."

One of her attendants went out into the corridor and returned with baby Liz. She carried the child up to the bench.

"Oh, for God's sake, I don't want it! Give it to *him!*" Once I was holding the baby, she continued. "You are sentenced to a lifetime of caring for this little nuisance, changing her diapers, feeding and clothing her, educating her in the corrupt ways of your wicked world, etc., etc. *Now get the hell off of my ship!*"

As she stomped out of the room, I turned to Sesbania.

"What in damnation was that all about?"

"I can't believe you swore in front of the child!"

"Sorry. Anyway, what was the point?"

"The trial? Partly to assuage Marpesia by having it on record that Eugenia's child is not yours; partly to satisfy me that your sins—both upper- and lowercase— are now all exposed; and partly for the sheer fun of putting you in fear of your life. Did it work?"

"Well, abject terror's been my ready companion for so long, I don't remember what it's like *not* to live in fear of my life."

"Don't be a killjoy—and you *will* change the diapers?"

"Oh, I'm looking forward to it."

As luck would have it, I got my first opportunity right then. Baby Liz had passed her own judgment on the proceedings.

I spent the night with them both in Sesbania's quarters.

"Do you remember when you visited me in St. Pierre?" I asked as we lay in bed.

"Yes, I remember."

"Why didn't you tell me then you were going to have a baby?"

"I... Well, I hadn't decided if I wanted you to know. But you did get the keys?"

221

"I assumed that was you. Yes, I got them—you saved my life."

I didn't see any point in telling her they were the wrong keys. Mainly because that would mean introducing my sojourn in the company of the accommodating nymphs. And this was about the only episode she was (at least, so far) ignorant of.

The next day, the three of us left *The Midnight Sun* in Miami and took the overnight express to New York.

We arrived in that city with just seventy-some dollars between us. By flouting the articles she'd signed aboard the Amazon ship, Sesbania had forfeited a sizable share of the booty she'd helped acquire.

"I don't suppose there's any chance you managed to hang onto that fifteen thousand you had on you?"

"What?"

"The fifteen thousand in assorted currencies you'd sewn into your chemise."

"Oh, that. Well, for the six weeks previous to my abduction, I had the stock listings from *Le Figaro* sewn into my chemise. The cash I'd deposited at a bank in Paris."

"In Paris? You were planning to give me the heave-ho and go back to France?"

"Let's just say, I preferred having that option. I'd hoped to retrieve it on Marpesia's next crossing over, but that never came off. That seaplane you had us chasing after was a dud."

"There are other means for going back."

"Are there? Well, then I suppose I'd just prefer not to. Wouldn't life there seem frightfully dull after what we've been through?"

"Not for me. My trial and execution would make sure of that."

"Trial and execution?"

"On my one trip back, I helped steal a Navy sea-plane. Plus, there was a gaggle of New York financiers hoping to hang me from a lamppost. And your dear guardian, the countess, had a pair of thugs out trying to track me down."

"Oh, dear," she said with mock concern. "Well, things will work out. They always do."

I wasn't feeling quite so confident. I feared her in-sistence, voiced earlier, that we both give up our careers of deceit would limit our opportunities too severely. But Fate was about to give me a powerful assist (though which one of them it was, I can't say).

What with my kidnapping by Bonnet, the nights spent with the graceful Euphrosyne and her furious sister Megaera, my reunion with Sesbania and trial by Marp-esia (not to mention the advent of apparent fatherhood), I'd forgotten completely about the public-relations efforts I'd set in motion down in Havana.

As it happened, my vanquishing of the fiendish Cy-clops and dispatching of the pirate menaces Jack Tigue and Jean Lafitte featured largely in that week's Sunday supplements. They included artists' renditions of both me and my victims, plus maps and schematics of the various airships.

I was an instant celebrity. And darling of both the rum-runners the pirates had preyed on *and* their vast clientele. On Monday I made a deal for my likeness to appear on some sort of breakfast cereal. On Tuesday, it was a brand of safety razors. Wednesday was a line of men's clothing, and Thursday, I believe, toothpaste.

Friday was given over entirely to my adoration. For the ticker-tape parade, Sesbania, the baby, and I rode in a carriage with both the mayor and the governor. At the conclusion, one gave me the key to the city, and the other an admiralty in the naval militia. Then came a reception where politicians, plutocrats, priests, and other cretins competed with one another to steal a bit of my glory via longwinded testimonials.

That tedium was nearly compensated for by the dinner that followed. Hosted by the rum-runners' guild, it involved a seven-course meal, fountains of champagne, and a stone Cupid who peed martinis. All quite impressive.

We arrived back at our hotel thoroughly exhausted. Sesbania had just taken the baby into the bedroom when I heard a shout of distress. I flew into the room to find her kneeling on the chest of an oversized intruder. In one hand she held the child aloft, and in the other a dagger pressed to her adversary's throat. A pirate mother is not one to be trifled with.

II

Only then did I recognize the trespasser as a myrmidon. And I knew but one myrmidon likely to be as submissive as this one.

"It's all right. He's my valet," I told her.

"*Valet?*" I took from her tone she had some predisposition against the species.

"Well, manservant."

I took the baby from her and helped her up. Achilles rose more slowly.

"I apologize for surprising you, madam. I was just arranging the master's shirts for him."

He spoke tentatively; the encounter had shaken

him. After handing the baby back to Sesbania, I took him into the sitting room and poured him a brandy.

"I never expected to see you again," I said.

"Oh? I'd no idea you were displeased with my service, sir."

"*Displeased?* The way you abandoned me in Curaçao?"

"I'd only gone off for a moment, sir. When I returned, you were gone!"

"Yes. Quite convenient. Frankly, I don't see much use in a spineless coward."

"Don't you, sir? Well, if you think about it, having a thoroughly spineless fellow about can serve a quite useful function."

"And what would that be?"

"He acts as a sort of canary in a coal mine."

"Ah. So the moment you disappear, I grab the wife and child and head for the hills."

"Exactly, sir."

Pretty spurious reasoning, I admit. But he *would* lend the home a bit of class. Plus, he knew how to put the proper crease in a pair of trousers, something neither Sesbania nor I had ever mastered.

"All right—but the wife will insist that you share in the diaper duty."

"Happily, sir. If you don't mind my asking, is madam really your wife?"

"Purportedly. And best to not bring up the others."

"As you wish, sir."

A week after that, I received a letter from Avarice's lawyers: she and her sisters were suing for divorce in Tortuga. All they wanted from me was written confirmation that I would make no claims against their income. I was even given visiting rights to the children. I signed the papers, and just ten days later, the divorces were granted. I was certainly glad to have that behind me. Sesbania wasn't one to carp, but the topic of my harem had been a sore one.

She'd gone out shopping the next afternoon when Kelso dropped by.

"Just in time for cocktails," I told him.

"Excellent idea. I've news worth celebrating."

"The Panic of '07 came off as planned?"

"As pre-ordained. Your three thousand's netted you nine."

He held out a sheaf of bills.

"Not bad. But I want you to take that to Port of Spain and give it to Myra."

"Left her in the lurch, did you?"

"Yes—in a manner of speaking. Can you do that?"

"Of course."

"And not gamble it away before you get there?"

"Me? I'm the very epitome of self-restraint."

"Sir," Achilles interrupted. "I wonder if I might have a word?"

Before I could answer, Sesbania returned and dispatched him to retrieve some packages she'd left with the doorman.

I introduced Kelso as captain of an airship.

"But didn't we meet years ago... on the other side?" she asked.

"Indeed, we did," he confirmed. "Must be ten years."

"Well, it's lovely to see you again. I suppose, being the captain of a ship, you can conduct marriages?"

"Actually, that's something of a myth...." I began.

"Shut up, Pluribus. He's a captain *and* he's from the

real world. That's as close as we're likely to come to an authentic wedding."

By then Kelso had put away five martinis, so was game for just about anything. Once Achilles returned, he and the baby acted as witnesses. It was no closer to an actual wedding than one performed by an inebriated barfly in a neighborhood gin mill. But it satisfied Sesbania, so it was wedding enough.

We toasted with a round of martinis—then I remembered Eugenia's parcel.

"That package I gave you to deliver..."

"Mission accomplished. By the way, that cousin of yours is quite charming. Or was, I suppose I should say." He seemed to ponder the problem for a moment. "Anyway, I bought copies of all her books."

"My advice is to drink heavily before cracking them open."

"No problem there. Say, I should get going. I sail for the Netherlands in twenty minutes."

"The Netherlands?"

"Yes, House of Orange and all that. Though I've yet to solve the problem of how to sell a tulip short. Well, 'til we meet again." He downed his drink and dashed out the door.

"What was it you had him deliver to your cousin?"

"Remember those books Emmie wrote? And how they involved Eugenia and her family?"

"Yes."

"Well, according to Emmie, they're based on a collection of manuscripts Eugenia sent her back in 1903."

"Had she even been born then?"

"Not quite. But these manuscripts—again, according to Emmie—were sent from the year 1959. Interestingly, this was all news to Eugenia. But she seemed perfectly willing to believe in the myth. While she traveled with the wives and me, she had occasion to read Emmie's books. And she had quite a few objections to how her kith and kin were depicted. So she wrote out some corrections and asked if I would get the packet to Emmie. Sometime before 1910."

"Sometime before 1910? How would you do that?"

"Kelso has a way."

"How extraordinary.... Do you realize, if you arranged to go back prior to some well-known event, say a market crash, you could quite profitably capitalize on your knowledge...?"

"For instance, a crash in the price of tulips in seventeenth-century Holland?"

"Oh... *Tulip mania,* of course."

"Excuse me, sir," Achilles interrupted. "It is on that very subject of Captain Kelso's investments—"

"This is hardly the time, Achilles." The misguided myrmidon seemed not to realize that my bride might look askance at my having sent nine thousand dollars to my former paramour. "Why don't you go put the baby back in her crib?"

"What's he talking about?" the bride herself asked.

"Money. He seems to want a salary."

"Not altogether unreasonable."

"Perhaps not. But what's the point of hiring an automaton if you have to pay him?"

"Doesn't seem like an automaton."

"Well, he's a myrmidon, and they're alleged to all be automatons. He's just not a very good one."

"I see.... You know, I was just thinking.... Sending back those corrections. Seeing as we might now only exist in your cousin's fictional world, what if by some revision she writes us out of the story?"

"I hadn't thought of that."

"No, one generally doesn't think of textual revision as a life or death matter.... Still..."

"Well, if it does happen, at least we'll go quickly...."

"And together."

"Yes, and together."

She gave me a peck on the cheek. "You know, I hadn't asked, but am I safe in assuming you went through my trousseau before sending it on to the countess?"

"Well..."

"Good. Then I assume you read the letter I'd written to my future husband."

"Yes—it sort of came unsealed, and...."

"Oh, I'm not angry. I'm relieved. It's important you are aware of... well, aware of what could *happen*."

She gave me a second peck on the cheek, then went off to take a bath. A moment later Achilles returned.

"Excuse me, sir," he said as he cleared the glasses.

"Yes?"

"It's about those arrangements you made with Captain Kelso. I couldn't help overhearing. The largesse you showed the former mistress—very commendable."

"Thank you, Achilles. But given the situation I left her in... on her own, with a baby on its way...."

"Yes, sir. That's what I wanted to inform you of. After your departure from Curaçao, I went back to Port of Spain. There I learned the mistress was *not* pregnant. She'd simply been served undercooked eggs."

"Undercooked eggs? I see. But still, she must have been devastated when I didn't return."

"Irked, I would call it, sir. And that only briefly. She soon took up with a couple of the Mamelukes."

"A couple of the Mamelukes?"

"A matched pair—twins."

"I see. That's what you wanted to tell me when Kelso was here?"

"Yes, sir."

"You might have mentioned it when you first arrived."

"Well, sir, I wanted to save you the loss of face."

"Ah... Of course, now that you've told me, I've lost face *and* the nine thousand."

"Yes. Very unfortunate. Will you be dining in this evening, sir?"

"No, the wife's made reservations. Celebrating the divorce."

We had an early dinner, then took in a show. Unfortunately, it was a play by Melpomene's protégé, Eugene O'Neill. He called it *Desire Under the Elms,* and it was every bit as depressing as the Greek original he'd stolen the plot from. We stopped by a supper club to wash the ashes from our mouths, and there ran into ex-seaman Woese. He was dressed in a tailored tuxedo.

"I take it the radio business has served you well?"

"Oh, yeah—or did. I've moved up to advertising. That's where the real money's being made now. I just signed a deal with the hottest act around. As a matter of fact, they'll be plugging those razors you've endorsed. The Limnad Sisters."

"The Limnads? You mean the nymphs who drive men to their doom?"

He laughed. "Well, I don't know about that. But they'll definitely drive 'em to buy razors."

I claim no expertise in the business of ballyhooing, but using the Limnads to sell safety razors was to squander their powers of persuasion. Back in the real world, they'd be hawking high-end resorts, or luxury automobiles.

Suddenly, I was reminded of something Gertie had mentioned, about how easily she had set herself up like the fellow in Twain's *A Connecticut Yankee in King Arthur's Court*. Why couldn't I pull the same stunt? I'd be thought a genius just by "inventing" some commonplace engineering from the real side. Such as the internal combustion engine Gertie herself had kept secret.

The only automobiles in fictional New York were little electric runabouts and those comical Stanley Steamers. Were I able to develop a line of gasoline-powered sedans, touring cars, and roadsters, I would dominate the market. Especially if I had semi-mythical sirens singing their praises.

I recruited Dombrowski, still working for Gertie in Nassau. Then contacted the lady herself—a far more delicate matter. If she would contribute her old seaplane engines, we could disassemble them and make blueprints. It required all my charm—plus a twenty-percent interest—to induce her to sign on. But once she did, she was an enthusiastic collaborator.

Next came the hurdle of fashioning our own parts. For that, I needed to recruit all sorts of help: engineers, metallurgists, machinists, etc. And in the meantime, introduce petroleum as a source of fuel. To do *that,* we'd need prospectors, drillers, and refineries.

I invested heavily in the project, as a positive outcome seemed assured. And though there were occasional setbacks (our first attempts at refining oil resulted in some very impressive pyrotechnics), by that autumn, we were progressing on every front.

It was then I received a quick succession of disturbing surprises.

III

The first surprise involved a parrot. Sesbania saw it for sale while out shopping and thought it would be a fitting souvenir of our days amongst the pirates. And would also keep me company when she took the baby to see another former pirate girl in Philadelphia.

The bird looked familiar to me, but I assumed that was because it belonged to the same species as the parrot that'd crossed with us on the airship known informally as Wilbur. Until, that is, it opened its mouth....

"Ahoy there, skeezicks!"

It was, indeed, that same damnable Knut, the parrot forced on us by the annoyed Norwegian fishermen.

"He's got himself a cabin boy!"

Apparently, the story that he'd been served in Emil's salmagundi was mere hokum.

"You know, it's almost as if he's speaking to you directly," Sesbania observed.

She found it all very amusing—at first.

"Now, how would you like a taste of a real woman?"

"Do you know who he's mimicking?"

"No idea. How would I know that?"

"Nothing exotic!"

That evening, while he was helping me to dress for a night out, I offered Achilles a hundred dollars on the condition the bird be gone on our return.

"You may depend on me, sir."

"We're sinkin', Captain! Davy Jones is callin' us home! Women and parrots to the boats!"

The damn parrot had heard us from the other room.

"And make sure it's dead," I whispered.

"Dead?"

"Yes, I don't want to have it popping up again."

Thankfully, it was gone when we came home that night, and its absence went unnoticed by Sesbania.

The next morning, I escorted her to the station for the train to Philadelphia, and on my return, found a postcard from Celia waiting. She told me that she and Elissa had opened a tearoom together up the Hudson Valley and that she hoped we might come for a visit. I thought her unlikely to embarrass me by divulging details of our past encounters before Sesbania—but I didn't feel certain enough to take the risk.

On reading the very last sentence, however, that worry slipped from my mind completely. Only then did Celia let drop what amounted to a domestic bombshell: Elissa was pregnant.

Why was this a bombshell, you ask? For the answer to that, you'll need to recall certain details revealed previously. First, Elissa had been thoroughly enamored of Jack, and had no doubt been faithful to him. So if she was pregnant, Jack was not—as I'd been led to believe—infertile.

Second, despite her claim to the contrary, I knew Sesbania and I had not done the deed at any point that previous summer. Also, she'd sworn she had never gotten nearer Smedley than was necessary to verify he hadn't my scar. Earlier, however, she *had* spent some time aboard Jack's ship. And they'd both been decidedly cagey when asked about what exactly had gone on.

Third, when we parted, Jack pointedly reminded me that turnabout was fair play. I had assumed he was setting my philandering against Sesbania's carrying on with Marpesia. But what if he was referring to my having gotten *his* wife with child, and he *mine?*

The facts spoke for themselves. Not only did Jack have the means and opportunity, he had all but confessed.

Though the revelation came as a bit of a shock, the palpitations passed quickly. Frankly, if I was to raise another man's child, better Jack's than Smedley's. And, after all, turnabout *was* fair play. Just so long as the child didn't develop that cynical sneer Jack was always sending my way.

The third disturbing surprise arrived later the same evening—an unseasonably warm one. I'd brought a lamp out on the terrace and sat down with an edifying book: *E. Pluribus Van Slyke: The Yankee Pirate-Hunter.* It was written by a dime novelist I'd met in a speak on 149th Street (fictional; in real New York, about 23rd Street) who could deliver sixty thousand words in the time it would take me to eat lunch. And best of all, I could have it at ten words a penny.

It was, as you can imagine, a gripping yarn. In the first chapter alone, I slew more pirates than greater Schenectady has people—and rescued more chaste maidens than Yonkers has chaste maidens. But while the swordplay was both dramatic and bloody, the lovemaking was thoroughly anemic. What's the point of rescuing chaste maidens if you leave them in the same condition?

I posed that very question to Achilles, who a minute before had been pruning a potted shrub, but I received no answer. I peered inside and noticed the apartment door was open. Perhaps, I thought (rather naïvely), he'd taken the trash out to the chute in the hall. But as time passed, the likelihood of that waned.

The answer to the riddle arrived in the form of a winged creature of recognizable pedigree. Even in a metropolis as vast and diverse as fictional New York, a girl with vipers writhing amongst her tresses and blood dripping from her eyeballs makes an impression.

"*I am Fury!* Prepare to suffer my wrath!"

"Is that you, Megaera?"

"*No!* It is I, Tisiphone!"

"Oh. Well, I'm pleased to meet you." I was suitably terrified, of course. But in my experience, the same rule applies to Furies as to strange dogs: never let them sense your fear. "Care for a drink?"

"A drink! *Fool,* I am here to wreak vengeance!"

"For...?"

"Crimes of blood! *You murderous fiend!*"

"Oh, that. I can relieve your mind there. It was all smoke and mirrors."

"Smoke and mirrors?"

"Yes, flimflam. And an extremely well-executed publicity campaign. To be honest, I haven't killed anyone. But if you could keep that under your hat, I'd appreciate it. The myth has paid off extraordinarily well."

I took from the display of her long, sharp teeth that she was unconvinced. I tried explaining again, in greater detail. But it was no go. I finally had to use other means to assuage her....

No, not what you're thinking—what a mind you have! All it took was a refreshing mint julep and a five-percent interest in Van Slyke Enterprises.

She changed into her normal self on swallowing her julep and I must say she proved even more fetching than her sister. She could not, however, hold her liquor. By the second cocktail, she was slurring words and drooling out the side of her mouth. With the third, she passed out cold.

A moment later, not surprisingly, Achilles appeared.

"Given that you were expecting the company of a young lady, sir, I thought decorum demanded that I absent myself."

"I see. And how was it you knew the little Fury would be stopping by?"

"Oh, just a vague premonition."

"Well, next time, you might share your premonition before taking it on the lam."

"I'll endeavor to do as you suggest, sir."

"In the meantime, you'll need to find her a hotel room. I don't think she's in any condition to fly."

"No, sir. I think not. Shall I take her to the Forum?"

"Yes. Tell them she's a princess and they should treat her accordingly. And make sure they send the bill to my office. I don't want to risk annoying her, or the wife."

I thought Achilles had done an admirable job of washing away any evidence of ocular bloodletting, but within minutes of her return, Sesbania spotted a stain on the Oriental rug.

"Good God, a bloody footprint.... Someone coming in from the terrace."

The rug had a busy pattern, in shades of red, so how she noticed it is a bit of a mystery.

"Lift up your right foot, Pluribus." I did as commanded—and signed my confession. "I want to know what happened. And I want the truth."

I told her just that. Had I revealed such a story two years before, she'd either have laughed herself silly or had me committed. But given what we'd been through, she found it only moderately fantastic.

When Achilles returned from retrieving her trunk and confirmed my account, her response was to call the Forum Hotel and arrange to meet the so-called princess for tea the next afternoon. The thought of my wife exchanging chitchat with an avenging Fury gave me a chill.

I did, however, reap one advantage with my forthright confession.

"Now, how about you tell *me* a secret?"

"What secret?" She looked worried, and her eyes fell involuntarily upon baby Liz.

"What was it you told Clem in regard to the countess?"

"Oh... that. Well, I doubt you knew of it, but several years back, a man attached to the Italian Embassy in Washington disappeared."

"Disappeared?"

"Completely. He was last seen dining at the countess's.... Need I say more?"

"You gave Clem the means to blackmail your beloved guardian?"

"Oh, blackmail is such an ugly word. I told her because no one but me and the countess's longtime manservant knew the truth."

"So it would offer proof she was you."

"Yes, proof that she was me... and a little leverage besides."

I felt that chill again. It wasn't solely what she'd revealed, but also the inscrutable smile she displayed during the telling.

Things went swimmingly that next year. Our assembly lines were churning out matchless automobiles at an amazing clip. And as other items missing from the fictional world occurred to me, I introduced those as well, such as reliable air brakes for railways. But also more prosaic products, like mock turtle soup—a very big hit, especially among turtles.

In addition to making us rich, my efforts proved a boon for mankind. Not only had I saved the lives of innumerable railway passengers (and turtles), I'd put the tearooms of the Hudson Valley within a few hours' drive from the city.

I also had my flops, of course. Fictional women couldn't see much use for restrictive undergarments—girdles and corsets failed miserably, and brassieres, they insisted, should interfere only minimally. My biggest error in judgment was born on the evening of our second Fourth of July in New York. They had the parades, and the picnics, of course. But then what? Oh, a dance maybe. Some heavy drinking. Nothing you couldn't find on an ordinary Saturday night.

Well, what's the Fourth of July without fireworks? And gunpowder so simple to produce....

As I say, not the wisest choice. I felt a little like the serpent who tempted Eve with that innocent-looking apple—assuming biblical serpents experience regret.

On the positive side, family life was a pure joy. Sesbania was not nearly so insistent as she had been in her pre-pirating days. Which was all to the good, because somewhere along the line, she'd developed a mean uppercut. As for baby Liz, she almost never cried. And, in spite of her lineage, only rarely cackled.

Yes, I was sitting on top of the world.

"What," I asked Achilles one evening, "could possibly go wrong?"

Strange—a moment before, he'd been standing right beside me....

FURTHER ADVENTURES

The characters featured in this trilogy appear in a number of other, equally curious, volumes.

Pluribus is introduced as a guileful twelve-year-old in the Harry Reese Mystery *Posing in Paradise*.

Sesbania debuts as a six-year-old in an earlier book in that same series, *Kalorama Shakedown*, and gives an encore performance at age twelve in *A Christmas Most Shocking*. (The latter book includes both an account of the German aristocrat's death which motivated the letter to her future husband and the letter itself.)

The authorial endeavors of Cousin Emmie, aka M.E. Meegs, are chronicled throughout the Harry Reese Mysteries, and most succinctly in *First Blush: A Meegs Miscellany*.

Jack enters as a streetwise seven-year-old in the M.E. Meegs novella *Peddlers All*, the second book of the trilogy titled *All's Fair, Mrs. Biddle*. He returns as a journeyman con artist in *The Circensiad*, now age fourteen and on the lam. In *Hush, My Inner Sleuth*, we encounter Jack in middle age—though he's hung up his cutlass, complaisant women are a continuing problem.

Eugenia, too, appears in *All's Fair, Mrs. Biddle*, but as a newborn, and therefore with little to say for herself. However, her young adult daughter plays a featured role in *Hush, My Inner Sleuth*, wherein the ill-named Willie at last meets her long-lost father—*or does she?*

www.ingramcontent.com/pod-product-compliance
Lightning Source LLC
Chambersburg PA
CBHW050030180626
46810CB00002B/648